Ara Iskanderian

Godless Hour

A Yerevan Tale

Gomidas Institute
London

ISBN 978-1-909382-68-8

Gomidas Institute
42 Blythe Rd.
London W14 0HA
United Kingdom

www.gomidas.org
info@gomidas.org

CONTENTS

Godless Hour

"Earth, and Hermes, and King of those below, send up Darius' spirit from below into the light! For if he knows any further cure for our troubles, he alone of mortals might tell their end."

– Persians by Aeschylus

Preface

The magical, the mythical, and the unreal — or, more politely, that which cannot ever be fully known — has always held vast appeal to me. With a childlike curiosity I wondered what place could possibly exist for such things in the real world, beyond the books and imaginations that contained them. Was there perhaps some secret time when the averted gaze of humanity afforded the impossible and unknowable things respite from scientific rationale, and the routing nature of all-cataloguing intellectualism? Surely there remain dark areas of the globe — *terra incognita* — so unknown to us that they might still be described as home to the fantastic by that wonderful phrase which, once upon a time, captured the impossible on so many maps: *"Here be dragons..."*

Perhaps in the absence of such locations, other shadowy places might exist, albeit on a less grand scale. Not so much in actual, physical places, but instead, places in time where the inexplicable, the unexplained, and the unknowable reside, and in which fantastic things still happen. The proof might be found in little clues that point to a lapse in time, evidenced by the sense of *déjà vu*, or an unaccounted-for, too-fast hour, which we brush aside indifferently with the banal "time flies." It is perhaps in these time lapses, in the lesser-known corners of the world, that the magical, the mythical, and the unreal —

the fantastic – still reside. For me, such *terra incognita* assumed the form of Armenia.

This is by no means exhaustive evidence or conclusive proof, but consider the impossible geography of ever-contorting borders that is Armenia. The country we might draw on a map exists in no atlas; nor does Narnia or Middle Earth, for that matter. Consider that taunting mountain, so intrinsically Armenian, so ever-present, but so unbearably far away; whether your viewpoint is from exile, or home, you can never reach the mirage. Then, there is the defiant history: as the plaything of so many empires, yet outliving all, Armenia although not alone in this fate, is certainly unique. Few Roman provinces continue today as countries. By rights, the tread of time should have pummelled Armenia into the historical dust that comprises the footnotes of history. It has instead been a form of alchemy for the country. That uniqueness is not easily distilled into words, but is perhaps best evidenced in the curve of the language's letters. That alphabet, too, is impossible. Sure, it tames a language, but exists for many as a mysterious cipher, more a marker of identity than anything practical. Although it is so instantly recognisable, its maze of angles compels us to confront the true beast in its centre; our own illiteracy. I, tellingly by the choice of English in recounting my story, am one such guilty illiterate.

This then, for me, is Armenia: a place that, by rights, did not exist beyond some pictures on the wall – or if it did, existed solely in my imagination. Many a school teacher disabused me of the notion that Armenia was anything other than a province of Russia. Yet consulting an atlas would reveal it to be a very real place; one with earthquakes, wars, and other bad happenings, all of which were easily overlooked or ignored by the rest of the world. The detractors say: "Can any good thing come from Armenia?"

The effrontery of being overlooked, and subsequent confrontation, is a constant theme in Armenian culture. Whenever an Armenian meets a non-Armenian, they are duty-bound to reel off the list of firsts: first Christians, first genocide, first shoe ... and we laud and loathe the list of greats all tellingly named "-ian." But this action Armenians perform is a great tradition with a fine pedigree. It was Movses Khorenatsi who implored the world to remember that Armenia, too, is a place with its greats; though often overlooked, it is nonetheless still worthy of note. Maybe consciously, or maybe not, William Saroyan echoed the sentiment when he talked of a small tribe of unimportant people possessing unheard music, unread literature and muted prayers as a preamble to his oft misquoted allusion to a phoenix-like Armenia.

It seems as though to be an Armenian requires one to martyrise and memorialise; forever thereafter, to remind and remember, all of which contributes to disbelief by the non-Armenian. We start with firsts and lists, then progress to pictures on walls of scripts and peaks, before concluding with the finality of stonework: churches and khachkars, though rarely statues. For the most part, the latter we keep to that secret corner, that fantastic place: Armenia.

This is a story about those statues coming to life in Yerevan during one of those time lapses when God looks the other way, and, in the event of something so fantastic occurring, what those statues might say. In writing this short story my challenge was almost a tournament of dialogue. In the imagined discourse of each statue, I sought to establish the following: from each of these greats worthy of memory in stone, bronze or steel, who would be the greatest overall? This was part of a personal challenge to answer my own set question: who should take the central plinth of Yerevan, which remains vacant ever since the deposing of Lenin's statue.

The dialogue that emerged was didactic and discursive, perhaps insufferably so, albeit with some well-known quotes here and there for the reader to mine. But as it emerged, the story began to serve a different purpose from what I set out to write. What emerged was each statue's account of their part in Armenian culture and history. I ask that the reader not judge too harshly the propensity to monologue, and instead enjoy the veneer of prose that coats those occasions of verbosity for what they are: a story of total fiction.

It might be said then that what the reader currently holds in their hands is a canter through the Armenian past, albeit with great gaps in between. It certainly should not serve as an overview; more like highlights, the choice of which was not made by me, but by whatever now stands by way of memory in the streets of Yerevan. True, not every statue in Yerevan has been brought to life; the great Mkhitar Gosh and genius Anania Shirakatsi fail to make an appearance, and some might note that Charles Aznavour's statue travelled from distant Gyumri. Lenin too, though still around, albeit hidden, is a contestable choice. There are also too few female statues to locate.

This then gave me my cast of characters, and what is more the manna of information from which I could construct my dialogue. To learn of these statues and the stories behind them was an education, even for me, a trained historian. Sure, I knew that Tigran built an empire and the greatest manifestation of Armenia, but I knew less that he was a Hellenophile, and questionably recognisable (at least culturally) to a modern Armenian. I knew too that Vartan had been king of Armenia, and a great warrior who had beaten the might of Persia, but I was soon corrected of these assumptions; he was no king, and he won no victory. The joys of this journey of discovery kept coming. Why was Armenia a fatherland, yet its father, Haik Nahapet lies on the city outskirts, whilst Mayr Hayastan, the embodiment of the neologism "motherland," looms so large as to be ever-present? The answer was simple: her statue had itself replaced an earlier statue of Stalin. If Lenin had been torn down, why not the statue of his Bolshevik comrade Shahumian? Perhaps the latter we retain because he is Armenian, and his fate, one of martyrdom, is appealing to Armenians. There were other mysteries too, such as, where was Charents' body, and is Arno Babajanyan's nose accurate, or a caricature?

Learning sometimes crashes against the rocks of imagination, and so I began to wonder what the legacies embodied in the memory of these statues might mean in the present. It was one thing to think of Tigran's empire or Charents' poetry, but they had mouths, and they could speak: what if they did so? Would Mashtots come to life and be as fussy about repeating the alphabet as a Sunday school teacher in meticulously making one tell the difference between the many consonants? Would Khachaturian immediately start composing again and finish his last manuscript? What about Saroyan? Would he tediously walk around Yerevan, banging on about triumphing over a tortured history? These playful questions animated my narrative as much as any message that may or may not be discernible in this book.

I ask indulgence of those readers who would demand a more exhaustive cast to remember that we are too expansive a people to make the cast complete. Instead, I hide behind the defence that the story is my own, and the choices reflect what worked for the tale herein to be told. I felt that each of the living statues, in being resurrected and speaking, could tell us something about Armenian identity, history and culture. Their long-dead voices might give insight into the current state of the nation, so to speak. For it occurred to me that the great dichotomy of the Armenian nation is an underlying tension between a territorialised Armenian, being all that remains of a much larger but lost Armenia, and the dispersed Armenian, which, far from being a motley collection of émigré, exile or migrant communities, is in fact a constant in Armenian history. Both survive by the same cultural adherence and tonal markers: longing, return, imagination, even — but certainly owing much to a thick seam of lamentation. For when the Armenian navigates that lists of firsts, greats and "-ians" in order to remind the world that Armenia is, and isn't, fantastic, lamentation serves as a compass. This provided something of a revelation whilst writing this book, and a common theme that could be found through the dialogue of my resurrected statues.

The ancient king who lost his kingdom is at once a shorthand for the Armenian experience. A maximalist Armenian state, briefly but proudly stretching from the Caspian to the Mediterranean, that we all know and speak boastfully of. Yet this same king was wholly illiterate of Mashtot's script and, like so many of us (including myself), knew too well how big Armenia once was, but remain less familiar with how rich and diverse the culture is. Should that tell us something? Perhaps that we are a cultured people whose fretting about borders has served us only in their shrinking, but whose cultural output is so great, that perhaps that is what we should focus on; lest we be as other observers of Armenians have warned, like a peacock - with the best parts behind us.

In discussing the relative greatest amongst our greats, I reached awkward conclusions that were not self-serving and may not please all, or even some, but I hope that they are taken for what they are - a challenge to think differently as to the many competing legacies and potential futures that comprise Armenia. In my greatest hope you might call to mind these dialogues next time you wander around Yerevan and use these statues as much for landmarks of Armenian history and culture as for navigation. All herein is fiction, except for those parts that are not, so I pray your final indulgence, and ask that to the text, please be kind, it was a labour of love, not scholasticism. The presence of Ajami is pure whimsy, partially serving as a master of ceremonies, and in equal part, a stand-in for that force that so regularly seems to conspire against Armenia being left alone in peace. Do not read too much into him. The illustrations are my own. They are no great works of art, but served to discipline my imagination, and I thought to share them rather than leave them to languish in the drawer. I have sought not to obscure the identities of the statues with the names I have given them, but should the real name elude you, a guide is included at the back.

I will end this introduction by saying that with each trip to Yerevan, the inspiration grew for this story until, one day I decided to take a pause from the vagaries of life, and write it down over the course of several weeks in a little tea shop on Abovian Street, which is now, like so much, alas, no more. I hope you will enjoy reading my story as much as I enjoyed writing it.

Ara Iskanderian

22nd July 2021, London

I

The Triumvirate

"If they are here as ambassadors, they are too many; if as enemies, altogether too few."

—Tigranes the Great

At the secret hour, well past midnight, the demon Ajami visits Yerevan on his nightly travels through the Godless dark. He laughs, and those still on the street feel a chill wind snapping at their bare hands, their noses twitch, and the napes of their necks shudder.

Wherever the few denizens of the city still awake quietly shuffle along, Ajami alights from his flight and whispers a lullaby. Although their stubborn ears hear nothing - only deafness meets his song, deafness and a tingle in the night-time breeze - they cannot help but hear the beckoning call of tiredness. Ajami does not care if they ignore him and continues singing his lullaby until an inescapable slumber compels even the hardiest among them to seek their beds upon hurried feet; there to sleep, and perchance, dream. And of dreams, what might come?

Fell shadow of creation, Ajami can bring stone to life through his play, and as he dances through the now empty streets, his rough touch and cold kisses bring the statues of Yerevan, the Rose City, to life.

A great Titan, barely hewn from the white rock of his pedestal, sheaves his sword, and solemnly paces towards

Ajami the Ever in Motion

the square where the great meet of Ajami's summoning is to take place. A weary brow ripples across his forehead, and his arms, all muscle and stony sinew, end in hands searching for non-existent pockets in which to bury themselves – they rest instead upon his girdle belt, granting him a determined look.

Illiterate, the Titan stumbles through streets seasoned with Latin and Cyrillic, and peppered with glimpses of Greek; the latter he recognises, from alpha to omega, but not enough to make sense of. Though, he booms silently in thought, was he not the King who engaged Athenians in rhetoric, only for philosophers to die of starvation? Did he not also recline in the entertainment of Ionian actors, before that gourmand Lucullus burnt down his theatre? If in these parleys with Greek he had shown himself able, then surely no language can stand before him now. And yet, of this new angular script the Titan sees about him, he is wholly ignorant. Its sight burns his eyes, whilst its sounds die stillborn upon his tongue. He greets it as he would any enemy; hubris shall be his sword, and arrogance his shield, nothing shall defeat him! The script, in turn, counterattacks, and quickly surrounds him. He is no great tactician, and the Titan surrenders, defeated, like so many schoolchildren from his day to this.

Ajami chuckles to himself upon the grey steps of the Matenadaran, whilst the Titan stumbles drowning in chalk, not learning his lesson.

Soon enough, Ajami parts ways with his mirth. Composing himself, the demon kisses the Lord of Words, who sits atop the hill in eternal counsel with the Learned Firsts, and the stone monk also comes to life.

"Behold!" declares Ajami to the newly woken Lord of Words, the demon outreaching his hand to point a spindly finger in the direction of the ambling Titan: "Your pupil awaits!" The Lord of Words rouses himself and stands upright, carefully smoothing the creases in his cassock, whilst his stoical face contorts anew, forming into a countenance of rebuke.

"Foul cretin Ajami! A curse upon you! Will you not let me rest in stone-wrought sleep? Why must you labour me more? Is not my time on this earth done? Let me sleep! Leave me in peace! Be gone!"

Ajami gestures to the forlorn Titan, who seeing his kingdom reduced, and his empire in ruins, struggles to pronounce an unfamiliar word: "*Han-a-rap-te...*" The Titan pauses, realisation floods over him: "*Re-poob-lik,*" he mutters. This word is suddenly unfamiliarly familiar. He understands it now.

This detestable word 'republic' is a disease. A Roman blight attacking the body and costing the head. How many lands fell afoul of its empty promises of freedom in place of glory, he asks himself. Now, too, his own native land lies in thrall to this infection.

The Titan tries to shake his head free of unhelpful thoughts; of battles won, and wars lost long ago; of his Roman nemesis, those self-same Romans who knew not the stay of mountains, nor of sea, in whose wake was left desolation. The Roman course was known by that name in all tongues, though in their own, they called it 'peace.'

To distract himself he turns his attention to his surroundings. Where is the square named for him, the Titan wonders. The square within which chariots and horsemen may race, or through which subjects may pass in supplication and tribute?

Why now do men and women gather and call for the ending of ministers and the fall of presidents, where once they called for the heads of Romans and corpses of Persians? All this, he contemplates, and more, as his once straight back, stoops, and his shoulders, broad, drop, whilst in his hands, his collapsed face he places, oblivious to the Lord of Words coming to sit beside him.

"Greetings!" says the Lord of Words, and the Titan nods, a begrudging acknowledgement – lonely he stands, lonely he would rather remain. "Let us begin the lesson," the Lord of Words says, and creaks open the stone book that he had previously kept tucked beneath his arm.

"'*Ayb, Ben, Gim...*'" The Lord of Words traces a fingertip over the stone pages drawing thick, black, angular shapes that appear like ink-blot stains upon the porous stone. From their fraying edges, the letters spread out across the pages, an ever-creeping shroud, threatening to turn into words and foreshadowing sentences.

The Lord of Words peers over them, like a proud father watching children at play. The Titan stares in turn. He wants the shapes to be familiar, just like the Cappadocians he once-upon-a-time conquered were familiar, but they are mute before his gaze, just like those very same Cappadocians were mute when they prostrated themselves before him.

The Titan waylays his stare and looks dejectedly into the unforgiving night of the Godless Hour, the playtime of Ajami. Old women, too blind with years, unable to see this secret hour, too deaf with years, unable to hear Ajami's lullaby, are bent, doubled over, back-breakingly so; they dedicate themselves to their task, and sweep the vacant streets clean of another day's history. In their place the Titan recalls images of Amazons, bows bent back, standing upright and straight, ready for his command... He drifts into dreaming...

An old man walks past. His bleary eyes, yellowed by tobacco smoke, have seen too much to not see the Godless Hour, and despite the ravines that course across his forehead, and the hairline that recedes like an ebbing tide, his face remains defiantly childlike; half-wonder, the other half, all moustache.

The Moustache approaches the Lord of Words and his pupil, the Titan.

"It is a good night to be alive!" declares the Moustache, throwing his head back and stretching his neck to the heavens, his body creaking in opposition, his face inhaling the night like a smoker. The Moustache's interruption of the lesson is met with muffled acknowledgement from the Titan, and an uninspired response from the Lord of Words, simply: "It is."

From somewhere about his person, the Moustache produces an old newspaper rolled up into a cone containing sunflower seeds. He offers them around, and the triumvirate sit and stand together not saying a word - only the sound of cracking between teeth breaks the silence. Steadily, the pavement is painted with broken husks and saliva-sodden shards, as a king, a monk, and a writer pass time eating seeds, like some preamble to a bad joke, only that the punchline is that the lesson continues.

The stone pages creak until they come to open upon a line of text, and the Lord of Words recounts the first sentence ever written: "To know wisdom and instruction; to perceive the words of understanding..."

It is a sweet song to the Moustache, who is lost within its cadence.

The Borders of the Armenian History Book

The Titan, however, discovers his voice, and ignoring the lesson, interrupts it with what is currently reigning in his head:

"When I was king, certain Hebrews, recently conquered, came to my court. I asked what tribute they had brought me. They pleaded that theirs was a poor land, with no swift horses, no wines of great repute, and no gold to offer me, but that in knowledge, they were indeed rich. I said that if that was truly their only wealth, then they should share with me certain passages of their texts, passages that would be worthy of a king and humbling of any Greek at my court.

"These words I hear you now speak are an echo through the ages. I know them well. But not for me, such trinkets! No! The deft sweep of a sword, the parting of my enemy's head from his shoulders that it might fall and thud in the dust and din of battle, these are things I understand, what I perceive, the wisdom I seek!"

Unimpressed, the Lord of Words shakes his head dismissively, and responds, "He who lives by the sword, dies by the sword!"

The Moustache gestures in agreement, though the Titan remains oblivious to him.

"Ah! But with one thrust, death is your gift! With one stay, life is returned!" replies the Titan, thrusting with his sword in a most violent action.

This time the Moustache responds:

"If the sword cuts well, they praise the arm. If the horse leaps well, they praise the rider. They—" But he too is interrupted.

"I was a king!" roars the Titan, standing upright suddenly, his chest pushed proudly forward and his arms, ending in clenched fists, stretching outwards. He turns his back to the Moustache and the Lord of Words, his rapt audience of two, who take seats and quietly return to the task of splintering sunflower seeds as they watch the Titan's performance.

"In my time I built an empire that stretched from sea, to sea, to sea..." The Titan's voice trails off slightly as he draws each coast mid-air with his index finger. "My table knew food from all corners. Asia was a banquet from which I might choose delicacies to sate my appetite; and my thirst was quenched by chilled spring waters each morning brought in amphora from many lands and poured into one cup, the cup of a king no less: enamelled in gold and studded with jewels.

"Incense and perfumes from Arabia filled my tents and pleased my nostrils, Greeks performed tragedies for my eyes alone, and wines as red as fire and stronger than iron bonds inflamed and calmed me in equal measure. Four kings were servants to me, indulging my every whim. King-of-kings they called me, and this my title became, for no commoner attended my table, nor kept my company, nor even held the bridle of my mount.

"I built a city from which to rule, and what a city it was: walls so high that even the towers of Ilium were surpassed, walls containing stables filled with horses - the fleetest, the swiftest, the hardiest" - he clenched his fists and punched the air - "and gardens, gardens full of fish ponds, and parks, parks filled with a menagerie of beasts, so much greenery... such greenery that the desert beyond blushed in shame and retreated before my splendour. This city, an eye from which to peer out upon my empire, was vast beyond measure.

"For had the ablest, strongest man in my realm, nay, in my realm and even beyond, pulled back a bow and fired an arrow towards the sun, and if, where that arrow landed, the fleetest horse started at a gallop and rode until it tired and collapsed from exhaustion, if even then the rider dismounted and walked until his own last breath, still you would not have reached an end to my domains!

"Why do you say 'A' and 'B', 'C', and 'D'? Speak not of letters, but of lands, holy man! For what use are letters, if not to construct words, and what use are words? Do they not exist firstly to record achievement? Record this achievement!" And he taps upon the Lord of Word's book.

"...Albania, Cappadocia, Cilicia, Medea, Atropatene, Judaea, Syria - all these lands, and more, I gathered unto my bosom having plucked them from the field as the ploughman would his harvest. My sword was a scythe unto the nations - let their names, my conquests, be your alphabet!

"When Parthians fired their parting shots, I gave chase that their arrows flew not far. When Greeks spoke loudly their heroes' names, I drowned their noise with my own greatness. No pirate in his Cilician cove, nor Medean in mountain abode, dared leave his hole without my say so. Not without good reason did they call me 'Great,' for speak now of your Nazarene Christ, and know that at my birth too a star did appear to mark the occasion. Speak again of your Hebrew Messiah, and I will tell you that had I lived fully unto the days due unto me, and had sons worthy of my legacy been born to me instead of the treacherous brood that claimed my name, then your Messiah, and all that came to be would have been within the confines of my empire - they would have said, 'Give unto Tigranes, that which is due unto the King-of- kings' and Caesar would have been unknown."

The Moustache, unable to contain himself any longer, and with a birdsong of thought, interjects, "And God did make the world so that man would know distance, and God made the Armenian to make a mockery of that distance." For emphasis he clasps his hands together and wrings them as though a wet cloth.

With his yellow eyes staring into nothingness he finds himself lost in the thought of fig trees. Fig trees in Bitlis, fig trees in Fresno, fig trees as far as the mind's eye could see... in Anatolia, in California... a potential harvest of the imagination dictating the seasons of his mind. Sometimes stories blossomed therein, like the first flowers of spring, whilst others withered and died smothered by winter's hoar frost, but for now his mind is an orchard of fig trees, an easy conquest for the Titan to add to his dominions, and this the Titan does.

The Titan's voice booms, interrupting the Moustache's thoughts. A mounted army rides roughshod through the groves of fig trees, which dissipate, smoke-like, from the Moustache's mind's eye, as the Titan's voice roars again. Reminisces, and pages torn from history, are now the staple of this Armenian's laments.

"My empire was like a pomegranate: taut, coloured crimson, the cities within as many as its seeds. The armies I commanded were vast in number, more numerous than the tears of those who came after me – those wretches who traded their forebears for forbearance, and in so doing, the sons and daughters of conquerors became the sons and daughters of the conquered.

"Ask yourself, holy man, was this faith you peddle, these words you smith in place of swords, were they worth what became of our people? Swords into ploughshares? Hah! What a pitiful notion to sell! The self-same stock that you turned into sheep for wolves to prey upon were those that marched to war for nothing less than glory. Who, when assembled under one banner, were as wheat in the field in number. And just as the wheat sways according to the wind, so they marched in unison to wherever my command ordered them to march that they might conquer, not to march that they might die! And when they marched, their march was boundless, only the sea halted them, and even then, if my Armenians had mastered timber and sails, then I would have added the waters to my domains as well. Even Rome herself would have trembled. King-of-kings they called me, bane of Romans, bane of Persians; Greeks called me brother, and Hebrews, saviour. Egypt stood, waiting, like a willing bride... Babylon would have been my footstool… Cyprus, my plaything... my armies..."

"Enough!" interrupts the Lord of Words, and the Titan, who had stood there beating his chest, calms from the crescendo of his monologue.

"Nation shall not lift up sword against nation; neither shall they learn war anymore." A stern gaze and wagging finger bring the Titan to total silence. "No more of armies and empires, these are they now."

A stone finger taps the stone book, each tap a chime of rock in rhyming unison to the letters that appear upon the page.

"An empire of letters now instead; each letter, a soldier, each sound, a chariot – see how they are armed and arrayed, cast over them proudly, with the eye of a general surveying his troops, that much should be familiar to you. Here are Ա and Ք, your vanguard and rearguard; Բ, Գ, and Դ, each a swordsman, three heroes ready for war, they'll make short shrift of paragraphs; look upon Ճ, Ծ, Ձ, and Ջ, four chariots to scythe through your thoughts; there are Կ and Վ, able slingsmen, to throw words, just see where they land and delight; whilst Թ cracks the whip, marshalling discipline for any pen. For cavalry come riding forth four horsemen: Ղ the charger, Ը the knight, Ի the lancer, and Ր the cataphract – see how these letters are men mounted on horses, heads biting at the bridle, what thought could ever outpace them? And look, shield bearers Ռ and Ո to protect the flanks; and for archers, I give you Ե and Է, look at how they take aim with straight backs, bow strings tautly drawn, and arrows at the ready, their flights are whole sentences in length; and for siege engine, I give you Խ, and Պ leads Յ and Փ, a column of war elephants, no wall of books will withstand them.

"This, this mighty King," says the Lord of Words, tapping on his stone manuscript, "this is now your army, who spill ink, not blood, who conquer books, not provinces, and who build libraries where palaces once stood. How fleeting the works of man, how quickly lost a kingdom, how immortal the words of man, how soon recalled a saying. Search within pages, mighty pagan King, and you will find your works, tales, and deeds written by these letters, by these soldiers assembled into

The Army Assembled

ranks, words are formed. They replace armies, nay, they do more, they defeat armies!

"For whoever heard of any emperor who sent men to war with words? Why no one! And what emperor, or king, who ever built great walls, conquered vast territories, vanquished great enemies, was by these deeds alone satisfied when the onset of death became familiar. Why, not one! All succumbed to words, all were defeated by legacy in the same way they were defeated by death. Their hubris, great in life, was greater still when the fanning breeze of their last breath concentrated them to one thought, and one single thought alone: 'Who will know of this?'

"All those greats are the same. They call out on their death beds, not for the swordsman to quicken death, but for the penman to delay it: 'Quickly, scribe, come hither and write my testament,' they all say in unison, and then in realisation, declare: 'My God! My God! Why have you left so little time for me!' Write, not ride, faster, they implore.

"Even you, King-of-kings, are felled low by such thoughts. See now on this evening how you bemoan fate, lament your former glories - why, do you not hear yourself? You wish that the world knows there was once a king worthy of note. These letters here, these are a gift to you, greater than anything you did build, all of which now stand only in ruins. These letters, they will be bards in your service, and structures to your legacy, far stronger than any stone, including that which is currently your being. All is dust that you left behind, no longer recalled. Take heed, and listen well, this will be your new kingdom."

The Titan, much cooled in temper, now stands in realisation, saddened that all his palaces and forts, all his campaigns and conquests, all the men who had marched in his wake or quivered beneath his raised brow, all were consigned to be forever hidden behind the meaning of this unfamiliar angular script. He ponders, and the rhythmic crack of sunflower seeds from the Moustache is anthem to his pondering.

With a subdued voice, he offers this to the Lord of Words:

"These letters are enemies, they are too many! And yet, if they are ambassadors of my deeds, they are too few."

The Titan's face returns to sadness, and the Lord of Words turns his tone to one more consoling.

"This new army shall in books tell of your empire, and all that came to pass within. Think not now of lands and satraps, ambition reined in by seas, but think instead only of these, the only mourners that will say, 'Once there was a King, and of this, his deeds...' Begin your lesson anew, once more now, this time with vigour: Ayb, Ben, Gim... A, B, G..."

"Ayb, Ben, Gim..." repeats the Titan.

The Lord of Words nods knowingly at the smiling Moustache, who in turn, smiles approvingly. "Now," says the Lord of Words, "repeat after me: 'To know wisdom and instruction; to perceive the words of understanding.'"

This time the Titan does not respond; he looks into the distance instead. Not for him these words, nor this army... he will forever dream of crumbled palaces, not unread literature. His pleading eyes set upon the Moustache, who encourages him with a look all benevolence and love, whilst the whiskers above his top lip and the mutton chops of his cheeks twitch and twirl, seemingly with a life of their own, a partial creature during the course of the Godless Hour, until the whiskers and chops come together to crown a knowing look that can no longer contain the smile erupting across the Moustache's face. The Moustache can bear it no longer, and he beams out a smile-borne sentence to the Lord of Words and the Titan, a sentence that has a poetry, though absent of rhythm, in full measure a harmony, and this he shares to the audience with him: "For when two of them meet anywhere in the world, see if they will not create a New Armenia."

All this, Ajami witnesses whilst laughing.

The demon comes amongst them: "Good!" he declares. "Not for nothing did I awaken you three first, for from you has come our motif for tonight. Let the Godless Hour of my playtime commence in full force, and this city's enslumbered awake: lamentations shall be our theme, however, that of so many children of Armenia."

With that, Ajami walks on, disturbing the lesson no more.

II
The Legacies

"Life is an island. People come out of the sea, cross the island, and return to the sea."

– Martiros Saryan

Ajami the Fell is birthed from libations, tears or wine, either offering will do; he is not picky as to what invokes him, only asking that he is invoked. Born again, he drinks greedily of whatever offering is made, supping on it with a connoisseur's delight. To him, both liquids are his elements, and they leave him drunk and giddy.

In this state he stumbles through the streets of the Rose City armed with a confidence that can only be born from an evening ill-spent at the wine house. In drink-sodden stupor, Ajami casts his life-giving-of-an-evening gaze over the Alabaster One, a great stone ghost, a trick-of-the-eye translucent, that haunts the dark and is invisible in the day.

Spectre, or spectacle, either way lifeless, and in being lifeless, colourless, save that where colour is visible, the being is coloured the self-same ivory of mothers' milk, on which, as in youthful life, now in stone death, to ween again, and be tonight restored to life. A cruel irony thus, his final rendition, so bland and uneventful, hardly the worthy epilogue of stone for one whose lifetime's renderings were a fantasia of colours.

There he sits, plain, this Alabaster One, aloof, alone, permanently suspended in inspired agitation, all hook-nosed and palette-at-the ready, poised to capture eternity in oil.

"Arise!" says Ajami.

The Alabaster One rattles to life, whilst his toga-like gown flows about his frame, an oversized canvas refusing to sit easily upon the easel that is his body. His wild hair, a nest of mother's blessings, tousled and white, stands on end in full defiance of the night-time chill, Ajami's constant companion.

He is an Olympian, out of place, and far from Arcadia. To no avail he tried to capture such antique scenes in life, this prophet of the pastoral, for now in death, as then in breath, he is as far from georgic scenes as his paintbrush ever was.

He sees in the Godless Hour something offensive to his long-starved eyes: the monochrome blanket of night. How violently he had fought for vibrancy, how loudly he had lashed out in oils, only for this single blanket of censored colour to rudely greet his reawakening.

His palette's captivity of colours is tonight made useless.

No need for vibrant blues, azure like the depths, never necessary those marine tones, for far from his mountain abode lay the sea. Neither, too, a place here for his golden yellows, or scorched aridity, no sun bakes the earth parched in this forgotten hour. The terrifying reds, mantles of ochre, vibrant and visceral, normally good for painting martyrs, are tonight not needed. More a cornucopia than a tableau of oils is this artist's tools, but on this night of fierce black, none will do to capture the petrifying darkness in which he appears to be framed, and to which any eyes that may see, may also forgivably think that the moon has descended from the heavens to spend a night on earth.

And on this night, the heavens thusly empty, having cast a funerary shroud to cover all colour, he plays the moon.

For in this Godless Hour, some lunar deity has come in the form of the Alabaster One to illuminate the unilluminable: his every footstep is a dull thud that teases hopefully, rather than command: "Let there be light..."

Not tonight the deepest blue, no golden sun warms the darkness, the brashness of purple and the verdancy of green are not needed in this hour, and so, as the monochrome blanket of night tucks away to sleep the colourful loudness of day's playtime, so too the Alabaster One, surrounded by darkness, rearranges his palette and stabs at its colours till they form a single mass of congealed black.

Now for a canvas! he thinks, and looks around him for what may serve, but his eyes' attention loses to his ears', which hear humming. The humming of something sweet and gentle breaking through the overpowering silence that is this blackest of nights.

A diminutive figure, almost dwarven in stature, appears from the endless mire - a small star to keep this descended moon company. The figure hums a tune of such beauty that the Alabaster One, fallen moon deity that he is, shines briefly brighter. His will be the light of tonight, made more radiant by music, ebbing and flowing in unison to rhythm.

As the song grows louder, the abandoned flower stall comes to life. Home to prostrate roses whose crowns are either the turbans of subjects bent double before their Shah, or pools of blood gushing forth from broken stems, the slain beneath their conquering Sultan, they are reborn, and the flowers, cut down in their prime, stand once more erect, defiant of both Shah and Sultan: in death, once more alive.

As the diminutive figure walks on, his evensong brings shop windows to life. Fruits reassemble into trees, lacklustre apricots are luscious once more, apples glow growing into fire – they're alive, and even a lonely pineapple, a stranger in a strange land, suddenly blooms magnificently. Mannequins dance in the old-fashioned way, like the parents who clothed them once upon a time used to.

The books in the windows of the tobacconist's shop come to life as well. Those of Bohemian writers, Kafka and Čapek, their otherwise unforgiving spines, now writhe like ecstatic Sufis, whilst their pages flutter in applause; a trial resumes, robots rise... even Freud forgives himself and joins the applause. As the midnight bard passes by, white whales breach twenty-thousand leagues of sea, whole worlds go to war to punish crimes and pursue peace, whilst the miserable and the miserly have chances renewed, again. Only Shakespeare stays silent; he will not be upstaged, even on this night, content in his dream-laden sleep to be a defiant corner that is forever England.

The Rose City comes to life once more and the diminutive figure's song continues, whilst the Alabaster One's moonlight, the serious moonlight, coats it all with his shadow, his incandescence a mysterious inverted dawn – "Moonrise has come!" the city appears to rejoice.

Yerevan awakes into slumber, living true to its name: it appeared!

The Alabaster One watches the Diminutive Bard bring the city to life, calling for colours once more, but his rejoicing is stifled. He mourns his palette, all too soon he had merged all the oils into one single mature black.

To be without a canvas is one thing, he ponders, to lack colours is a double crime.

To be an artist with no art is to die two deaths, and what passes for his soul sinks into the mausoleum that is his stone chest.

A lonely old man, gnarled and broken by years, walks by. He clings to a basket full of freshly cut roses in the crook of his arm; each crowned in bright red, they have been resurrected by the Bard's singing. The Gnarled Old Man's task is to deliver roses to the beauties of this city, but here, in the Godless Hour, such sculptures are few, and beauties, in his estimation, fewer still. So, lonely, he wanders in search of a deserving recipient until, tired by his futile quest, he pauses to rest awhile beside the

Alabaster One, there to gather his thoughts and bask in the fallen moon's light.

"A rose?" offers the Gnarled Old Man, and the Alabaster One admires the crimson red covetously before gratefully accepting.

Any colour will do for him, so long as it breaks the monotony of black on his palette.

Tenderly taking the rose by the stem, less a hitherto absent thorn should prick his fingers, the all too human part of him forgetting his stone-calloused fingertips, he gently places the single rose upon his palette, and then, recalling a mother's recipe for rose petal jam, he wonders if this same alchemy might birth a new paint for his brush.

Ajami the Ever-Obliging catches the whisper of this thought-cum-wish, and grants it instantaneously. Rose petals melt and merge, congregating into a thick oil, crimson red and juxtaposed against the incurable black.

Armed now with red, the Alabaster One sets out in search of a canvas.

The Rose City, in full thrall to the wanton abandon of the Godless Hour's spring, is now a cacophony of sound and vision, till even the Architect can no longer sleep, and so he too, with Ajami's drunken kiss, awakens to take heed of this dawn before daybreak, and therein, to resurrect an old friendship with the Alabaster One.

A new trio meet: the Architect, the Alabaster One, and the Diminutive Chanson. Together the three assemble before the granite grey of the Opera House, a great coliseum, enclosed by a roof, not for the gods peering down to know what happens within, no, secrets therein remain for not all the world to see. Here, the gathered trio are guests of that great seated colossus, who is even now still in slumber. The colossus is every bit as gargantuan as the Alabaster One, but ebony to the ivory of the former, and as these two giants meet each other again, the colossus rouses with thoughts of piano keys, black and white, and ink on parchment compositions, black and white, of this moonlit night, it too black and white, and though his vision is coloured thusly, it was he who brought to life sabres and Lezgins, dances both, waltzes that are fanfares to the cosmos, and operas to gladiators doomed to die before Rome. The Ebony Maestro is now awake too.

The Alabaster One, seeing the Ebony Maestro stir and crack his weathered knuckles, recalls once more his own calling. And as one wants for a canvas, the other longs for a piano - two artists without the tools of their trade instead exchange a silent greeting.

For what is left for the artist without his canvas, or the composer without his orchestra? Why, words alone, and neither are much known for these. They eye each other, night and day meeting - a silent all-too-knowing dialogue breaks out between them. Contemporaries in life, what conversations remain unsaid from then, to now be said as contemporaries in stone? Little save rivalry.

So instead, they stay muted. They are joined by an interloper.

The Architect draws near and breaks their muteness by soliloquising thusly:

"This is my creation," he declares, his dull eyes following his caricature-long arms as they sweep out across the city blanketed in darkness. "A dusty locale of no importance, beyond all that ever mattered, and far from all who might care, save those who sharpen swords and beat shields with their hilts. Small and meek, it inherited our earth!

"Most loyal of Armenian cities, only this bride remained wedded to us, whilst all the others forgot their nuptial vows, and in so doing, took new lovers, and in the adulterous embrace of those new lovers, all those faded cities remain as such: whores, best forgotten! Wedded anew, they are of a faded glory, silent of the tongue that called them into being, and filled not with the children that would have made of them paradises many. Leave them there, weeping by so many rivers, wanting for a song. Only my city remains, and see what a centre I have made her. Noah said it appeared, but I called her into creation!"

His hands play with shapes in mid-air, mockingly, his gestures are momentarily that of a maestro, and then affecting an artist's paint stroke, together conjuring a town.

"A city of concentric circles fanning out from the retina of this coliseum." He points at the Opera House. "See it now, this house of music, for what it is in my imagination:

a pebble dropped in a lake whose outwardly pushing ripples are the confines of my design, my Yerevan!

"It is a solar system this city, and here is your Sun." He points again to the coliseum before continuing.

"And each street is the circuit of an orbit, each landmark thereon that street, a planet dancing in its revolution, like the circles of whirling dervishes, an eternal circle within an eternal circle, each edging outwardly until the hills give it bound - see now the genius of my design, and revel in its labyrinthine intricacy, to be lost is to be a Theseus hunting his Minotaur, and I alone, an Ariadne, holding the string." He taps the temple of his stone head emphatically.

"Look again! Not askance, and see my works you mighty fellows! Despair! You who once lived, you who once lived here! Lived here, and when asked, turned your eyes to my temple, my Yerevan, and said 'home', you all who looked here from your dusty Baghdad, your Persian palaces, your mansions across the sea, and longed, sang and prayed to it as though your Mecca, you all were supplicants to my loyal, my beautiful Yerevan.

"It is I, the Grand Architect, who saw rest on every side, and who saw the staying of every adversary and every misfortune, and here built a house for the name of our people in which to reside. Here is your ark of gopher wood, not atop some distant mountain that mocks us with its gaze daily!

"I am that genius who built a city where once a dusty town of no import sat in the shade of shahs, and tsars, and

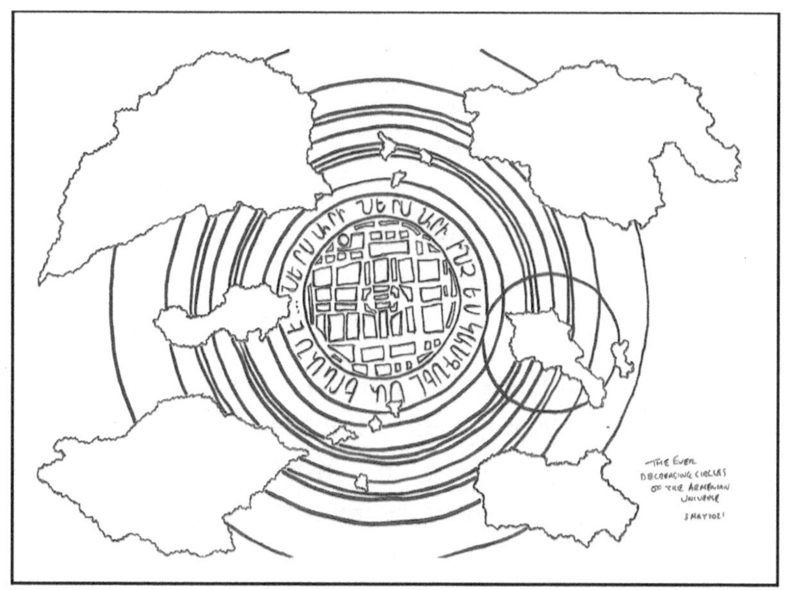

Ever Decreasing Circles

swords and scimitars! Not for me the mud bricks of Egypt, nor cedars of Lebanon, keep ziggurat and pyramid, baroque and all that the engines of the new age whose wet nurse is the new world conjured – I needed not to imitate Babel and scrape the sky. For from the sweat of my brow and the weeping of my pen, a new city was birthed of tufa and rose-hued stone that sweats in summer and cools in winter, truly it is a marvel.

"Look on my works Almighty, and say unto Solomon, he has surpassed you, for verily, I tell you even Solomon in all his glory did not achieve such a feat..."

Ajami applauds the boasting and chants, "Encore! Encore!"

The Architect duly obliges. "Truly I am great, for in the erasing of history, I banished History! Walk these streets and you will meet yourself along the way; my paths go on, they have no end. I have made here an eye, a wheel, nay, a revolution is my Yerevan. It sees all, it forever turns, and it will forever better! Compose and sing, paint and draw, write what you will - but colours fade, orchestras tire, and books from bookshelves drawn, to bookshelves return and remain unread again. Only the stone hewn, the stone-wrought remains...

"Look now, my brothers in endeavour, look now, and quickly so! Look now at us here assembled, and tell me, do not my rock-truths make sense? For it is upon my foundation stones that our church was built, whereas our land, before me, was but an altar, and our sufferings therein were as offerings to God above, and it was not a pleasing odour.

"No! Instead of altars to place your scribbling and sketching upon, like sickly suppliants placing offerings and pleading for attention, for you, a temple I have built, one in which you place paintings as though icons to be revered," he says, pointing accusingly at the Alabaster One, before turning to the Ebony Maestro, "and in which your music serves a choir, rather than a shepherd's flute. Both of you sit beneath the roof of my house, in which there are many rooms for all to come in and live, for all those who would dare to call this 'Home!' it is that, but in so doing, declare me a god!"

Grudging nods of agreement from the Alabaster One and the Ebony Maestro meet these bold claims. Ajami encourages the blasphemy to go on: "Speak more, my brother, for verily whoever sheds such words as these, he today shall be called my brother!"

Ajami cackles an unseemly sound before beginning his wondering anew, saying: "What is the truth, if not that which is set in stone?" His rhetoric serves as manna for the feral dogs of the city who now gather in packs at his heels, for this is a time for the unloved, and so, it is their hour too, and they bark in unison a chorus for any ear that will listen:

"From rock wrought stone;
A truth is borne"

And as fleeting as their arrival, so too is the departure of Ajami's party. Their night is to be that of tracing the circles of the Architect's imagination.

For the Ebony Maestro, these midnight denizens are in the moonlight hounds no more, but men in place of men. He looks at the pack of dogs fleeing and calls for their return in his mother's tongue. From these ruffian waifs and strays he will prove the Architect wrong - and that there are things more everlasting than stone, and this he will provide, if only Ajami the Broken will oblige.

Ajami the Revelrous hears the Ebony Maestro's prayer before his stone lips part to utter it, and with a fierce howl from the demon, the city's dogs assemble in attentive rows before the Ebony Maestro, who eyes them warily, drawing their attention.

"Now watch, oh Great Architect, and see that legacies are as much borne in song as rock-hewn!" And with that challenge, Ajami the Enabler magics a baton into the

The Dog Orchestra

Ebony Maestro's hand. With this, the maestro taps to attention the great pack of hounds before him.

"Wave, my son, this your wand, wave above the heads of these dogs, and see what magic comes," implores Ajami, and with a flourish of his wrist, the Ebony Maestro obliges, blessing the chorus of dogs as a priest does his congregation.

Here, where sons of wolves once roamed, instead there now sits to attention an orchestra: tuxedoed and bedecked with all manner of instruments; here violinists, and there cellists, oboists, and clarinetists occupy a corner. For the smallest pup, a triangle is given, and the gruffest, most bearlike of their number stands before kettle drums with a Turkish brow and Cossack moustache. Should there be need, and need in advance known, Ajami calls to life the Proboscis, sat on the shores of swan lake and peering, in spite of his ample trunk, downwards to survey the length of a discordant piano, the keys of which play cacophonously, as though a hammer's tap upon anvil.

"Now listen, Great Architect of tufa, and see what a composer can bring forth from the intangible, which you weigh and measure so affordably cheap! For as you erased history in stone, so did I lighten its burden upon our backs in turning it to sound, making the burden lighter than air. Behold and heed that anthem of our people: sabre dance!"

The Ebony Maestro ushers calm, and silence obligingly descends across Yerevan. The Architect, the Alabaster One, and Ajami make of nearby steps an audience's seats.

The Ebony Maestro conducts his Dog Orchestra as they play the fiery tones of Sabre Dance, and where the Bard brought shops to life, now the city itself has a soul conjured by the flicks and waves of the maestro's baton. For now the Architect's concentric circles spin in alternating orbits, clockwise, and anti-clockwise, and as the sabre dance spins itself to a close, a masquerade takes its place.

A lone street breaks the encircling circles and forms into the line dance of yesterday's peasants: they dip knees, perform hops, and with fleeting foot form an absorbing rhythm.

Behind this line of dancers dances a knot of streets, moving in the style of dervishes, and in turn, behind them balcony railings belove themselves into couples who dance above the heads of those street- bound.

The whole city has become a melee of movement: each distinct, all in unison, it is as though the forgotten sons of the dusty village that once was Yerevan have come forth from the underworld, seeping upwards through the paving stones' cracks, or descending from the stars above to the streets below, all to make a mockery of the Architect's utopia and dance to the Ebony Maestro's tune.

"Come forth!" calls Ajami to the shades of yesteryear, and ghosts obligingly appear. His own medley of fitful ecstasy and rapturous writhing has led him to dance alone on the top of the coliseum, but now, not satisfied, he calls others from hell and heaven to fill the dance hall that this city has become and to find amongst their own, partners with whom to dance.

Bolsheviks clasp Ottomans tightly to their breast, and waltz about; Soviets meet Safavids, and together reel and writhe; Assyrians delight Babylonians with fleet-footedness, only to be outdone by Persians and Urartians performing movements defiant of description. Here too come Romans and Greeks, Arabs and Macedonians, Byzantines and Mongols, each brings their own bloodletting dance to this cacophony, till a rabble of would-be conquerors all come forth to dance in discordance with another, but all mesmerisingly in tune with the music still playing.

Their unboundable clamour pulls the buildings at their seams, their marching, maddening footsteps such a

The Dancers of Yerevan

thunder that the Architect's eyes widen with fright that an earthquake may now school him in how fleeting any of the works of man are to the whim of nature.

The whole world now dances in Yerevan's crowded streets and shakes the city abed, for even the deepest human sleep stirs a little and wonders if this is it, if this is the end? But Ajami the Ever-Attentive assures those slumbering, assures him, assures her, that they are only dreaming of a Godless Hour, and that such a thing cannot possibly exist. They turn in their beds reassured and return to sleep - a passing nightmare is all, nothing more, they are consoled.

The dance continues until the whole city is one whirl of history and terrifying noise - such a pandemonium of dancers at once commanding attention, then dividing them in turn, all answering the call to "Come in! Come in!" To return home.

By now all the ages have merged into one mess, and all are here, ethereal spirits together, a conference of conquerors, an alphabet of invaders.

Upon flicks of the Ebony Maestro's baton, nations organise themselves once more into nations, in tune with cadence and metre, each appointing a leader with every new crescendo - here marches fierce Assyrians before their Ashurbanipal atop his camel howdah, and whilst Cyrus marshals Persians from horseback, his grandson gathers Safavids from his grandfather's ranks to fight under a new banner.

A Sultan calls his Seljuks to reign in their parting shots, Mongols look for horses as Timur calls them to his side, a Pompey rallies ranks of legions, and an Alexander forms a phalanx, each to their king, save the Godless Soviets and Bolsheviks who stand trembling under the wretched smile of the Kremlin Highlander whose mouth is toothed with gulags and whose cockroach moustache prepares to feast on carrion.

They marshal themselves these armies, each in turn, each ready for war, a dance no more, and as spearmen form to meet cavalry, and muskets take aim at archers, before swords can crash against sabres, the Ebony Maestro flicks his wrist abruptly to signal an end, and with one flourish, as quickly as all who had once upon a time been had appeared once more, just as quickly, all comes to an abrupt end; all is silence and stillness once more. The spirits return whence they came, and the city in full motion, now to a slow returns, as Ajami calls back the orchestra of dogs to their roaming.

"Now," says the Ebony Maestro, "are stones really all that remain to tell of truth? Does not the music I compose speak of ages past, and in it too a truth therein lies? Is there not proven to be much more that can speak of the past than just these stones and rocks of which you are so fond?

"For in their setting, they exist only to one day be ruined. Still they are born, and lifeless they remain, but music is *of this*, for true it is, that unplayed on script, it remains worthy of note alone, as lifeless as stone, but when worthy of note, it is note for note played, and thereby, it comes alive again. So as for your works being immortal, true, I can find no fault with your argument, for in all weather they stand, but in all weather and at all times they are alone, lifeless, whereas my work, to life one day returns.

"A wonder to the eyes you have certainly made, but to the ears nothing great. For stones no more make sounds once chisels cease their chime, save when in broken rubble, stones once more return to lie strewn, and amongst them people gather, mourn, and lament their ruin.

"Mark not too much your great works there, oh Great Architect, caller forth of creation, for just as easy a foundation stone, from the same matter a gravestone is hewn. But to the wasteland and back, to war and back, to the ends of the earth, and back, a song one can carry, and spirits therein raise, whilst the boulder tumbles from mountaintop thus" – and his ebony fingers play a chord in mid-air illustration – "awaiting a new Sisyphus."

The Architect bows, but unwilling to admit defeat, struggles momentarily, before carving a response. He points once more to his coliseum and feebly offers: "From stone comes this! Your home of rhythm."

"But for music, what need of this?" asks the Ebony Maestro rhetorically. "All the stone structures of the world are empty echo chambers in the absence of music. All structures, grand and great, and perfectly maintained, are but ruins in the absence of the sounds of man."

The Architect ponders this sombrely before responding: "And without stone structures, what place is there for music?"

"Then we are in agreement," offers the Ebony Maestro in a conciliatory tone. "One hand cannot clap alone! Stone calls for music, to bring its reason for being to life, and music calls for stone lest it die in the mouths of the wind. For even the voice that cries out in the wilderness calls for a home, if that home be only an ear that listens, so be it, but then let that same ear be housed beneath a roof stone, a rock upon which to build operas, orchestras, choirs..."

As the Ebony Maestro trails off in his sermon, the Architect turns to the Alabaster Master: "And what bring you to this discussion, painter serene?"

The Alabaster One breaks free from his quiet and unleashes a readied response: "Aye, the truth can be set in stone, and there it remains, lifeless it stays so - less by magic it is brought back to life. It remains in normal hours only a dead testament: fixed, immovable, true, but petrified as well, as much a gravestone as a structure.

"But in art, in song, in music - long after those creators are dead, these things remain in life: vibrant, living, playable, enjoyable - a feast for ears, and eyes!

"Yes, the truth is set in stone, unflinchingly so, but blood passes through art in every dash of red, as a pulse beats through music, these things can never truly die. But fleeting is music, for it hath beginning and end, and therein, its pleasure lies, but the captured image, stone-wrought, on canvas bought, has only alpha, and no omega. Its play has no end, nor need it rock even, colours remain at the forever dawn of their inception, if their home be made upon canvas.

"Now what is stone, if not the means of shelter, and with it a tempting target for envious eyes to look on, to covet, and to destroy - does history not teach us this? Why, of course!

"And when the stone structures the invader attracts, and they are reduced to rubble, for that is the fate of all cities, then too is truth proven that those that die are a reminder of the fate for those still alive, and then when once more people to flight turn, they will weep beside rivers and in strange lands, sing their songs of old, but with age these too will fade in the memory and die upon the tongue. For music unplayed is as a city uninhabited: without purpose.

The Never Ending Circular Argument

"But snatch a glimpse of memory, and with it imagery, and colours flood recollection with full vibrancy, and this herein I tell you is the purpose of art; to truly keep alive that which is fleeting. And what is more fleeting than our people, whose fleet-footed, unwearying tread takes them far from home, with its rocks and songs, and in exile, to dream muted dreams soundlessly coloured.

"Let us not long our hours with idle talk of whether stone, or paint, or song is the most eternal of arts, but instead, let us three agree to set aside square, brush, and baton, and say in one unified voice that to live again in this Godless Hour is a gift, and one not to be spent in arguing who is the greatest, but to instead say in living once more, albeit briefly, in such a time we can again create."

But the plea is met with deafness and defiance.

"Recall", says the Architect, "that we stand now here in stone! Keep your colours – what use are they in a city of stone that changes colour! What use is music to the ears of a nation who only wants shelter?

"Do you not see that we are of my city self-same made? Not paintings, nor muses come to life, but stone statues stand now debating – this is proof enough that I am the worthiest!

"For of my art a city was brought forth, and by the hand of a scion of my house, a sculptor did make you. Your breath now is proof that I am the best of three. Agree and let not our debate measure this night! You are statues of rock, self-same this abode; citizens of my city, forever destined to remain."

Two other heads shake. They will not agree.

So, the Architect, the Ebony Maestro, and the Alabaster One are doomed to spend their resurrection debating which of their three arts is the greatest, agreeing amongst their number only to agree to disagree, and thus proving that from three can come four, thereafter, five and six.

Thusly it continues, until even Ajami tires of their dialogue. How boring, he thinks, a composer without an orchestra, an artist without a canvas, and a stubborn architect whose work is done.

Ajami the Bored takes his leave and leaves opinions to waste time.

III

The Ashoughs

"No gratitude to my mother I feel, to my father's grave no duty is owed."

– Avetik Isahakyan

Ajami the Reckless locates himself atop the minaret of the Blue Mosque. From the spire he casts his eyes out across the Rose City now fully enraptured to the Godless Hour of his playtime.

The streets are far from full, and further from empty.

In the distance, he spies the Goatlike Poet walking lonely by, all besuited and nineteenth-century, hands clasped behind his back, appearing hunched over and as though his goatlike eyes are fixed on each proceeding footstep rather than glazed in thought. This tragic man betrays nothing; his visage is as hidden to meaning as any line of prose he conspired with ink to write.

The Goatlike Poet walks in a most contemplative manner, and at a most deliberate pace, he is consuming paving stones with his steps as he walks down a lonely street to a lonelier school where the torso-less bust of the Noseworthy One writhes in agony atop his pedestal wanting for a body.

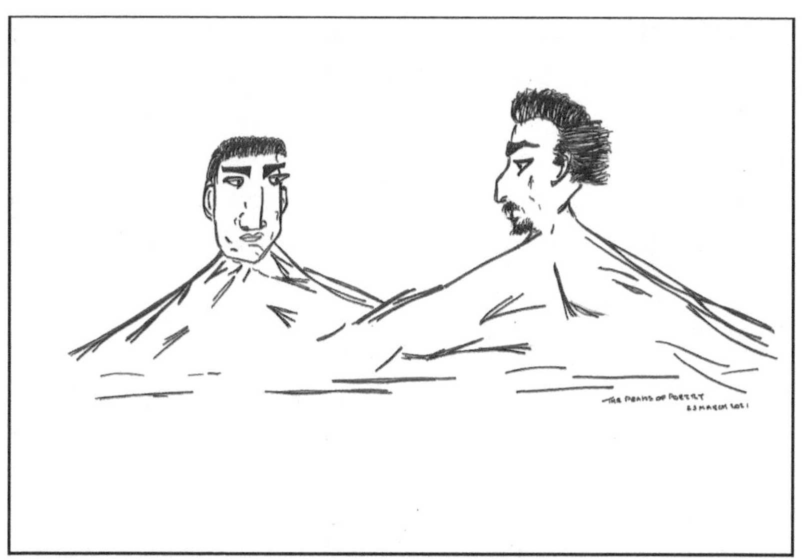

The Peaks of Poetry

In the hour of Ajami's play, the demon concocts his latest plan: he will conspire to create a duel of words between two greats of this mountain people, and in their fencing, Ajami will declare one a winner. Oh the joy, it escapes Ajami's chattering teeth and echoes like the rapid fire of crows cooing "carrion".

The Goatlike One greets the benosed torso: two poets, friends of yesteryear, but whereas one laid down his pen to rest in latter years, the other took up the baton and wrote words of sun-ripened sweetness.

They greet each other like Father and Son, exchanging weary looks. The fate of their race of poets being not to see a natural death, the maelstrom that is their country's history denies lettered men such pleasures.

The Goatlike One, paternal, speaks gently, if only to better hear the willed-for interruption he hopes will escape this son of his, this son whom he outlived, not in years, nor in time mind, but outlived by that very greatest act of defiance possible amongst their cursed readership, by dying naturally in bed. The Nose, well, who knows how the Nose met his fate, such things are best left mysterious.

Now Ajami sets the task at hand, question, of these two champions: who is the greater? Ten of the Noseworthy equals one of the Goatlike, but who often has the Goatlike in his wallet? Either way there is no money in poetry, though there is poetry on money.

The two poets exchange lines of verse by way of greeting.

The Goat goes first: "Oh, how little it is if I die with one life - would that I have a thousand lives!"

"But Brother," says Ajami, who alighting from the minaret above suddenly appears from the black mire, "has stone not given you immortality? And have I tonight on this night not given you a thousand lives, and one life more, that you might die again at dawn?"

He is answered with the Goatlike One bleating a line of his own verse: "Softly along through the hush of night, like a gentle stream's soft murmuring song." And joyful visions fill the Goatlike One as he watches the lines get lost in the audience-less night of the Godless Hour, his wispy beard of stone gently caressed by the beginnings of a cool breeze.

Unsatisfied by the response, Ajami turns to the Nose. "More opulently than your father now, O Noseworthy One, speak!" commands Ajami of the torso-less nose, bored as the demon was of the Goatlike One's melancholy ode to the night rather than to the fulfilment of his wish to live another life.

The Torso-less Nose looks in vain for the sun, veiled in the funerary shroud of a starless night and these words he summons forth:

"I love the sun savoury words of my sweet muse Nairi, but what use these words on a sunless night? Better I keep my counsel, measure instead words unsaid, and in so doing, pass the hours waiting for the dawn, there in new light, sun tasting words, inspired once more, be said." And with this, his neck cranes back in seeming agony, striking a humanly impossible right angle, his nose breaks a peak in the night, a new mountain to replace that one hidden from view.

"Is this what poets do with the gift of new life?" asks Ajami angrily. "Muse on naught? Compose nothing new? What curses can I lay at both your pedestals in lieu of wreaths, in place of blank sacrifices! I am your master who has brought you back into life; you who are worth ten of him, speak!"

"Nothing!" says the Goatlike One.

"Nothing?"

"Nothing, my 'Lord' Ajami," says the Goatlike One with no little hint of irony in addressing his Master.

His arms remain clasped behind his back, his face, a look of perennial contemplation.

"Speak again, tragic poet, for nothing can come of nothing."

But the Goatlike One moves not and instead he stays, steadfast straight, as though once again the true visage set in stone that he was last night.

Ajami the Soulless raises a hand to strike the ingrate old goat, but catches himself and instead turns to the Nose. "And what say you? Speak keenly, and swiftly, that this dialogue might make new life for you both. Speak of sunny words, chime them to the tune of old instruments, intone! Call forth ancient beauties, and in their gaze, be inspired to call forth such things that I might be appeased for the troubles I wrought in alighting on this city, of all cities that I might descend, and blessed with this hour, and brought the dead to life - come, oh Great Nose, and sneeze a little. Even in that trickling dribble there will be some delight, lest all those who walk past you, quote you, wax lyrical of you, be proven wrong, and instead that man of steel and cockroached brow and slug moustache be proven right, that you are so worthless in life that only in death do you serve any purpose, an example to fall aright of, and not to follow. Again, I say 'speak', and measure in metre well now, oh Great Nose, that I do not implore, but command you: SPEAK!"

And the heated tone of Ajami warms the wintry air before he finds himself and calms himself from his wild raving, composing himself into a more subdued form once more.

The Noseworthy One turns his impossible head to Ajami and defies him:

"Sir, I am made of the self-same stone as my brother here is, warmed and cooled by the same winter and summer as he. Though much might be said to separate us, and years and style would agree, he and I are of one mind: stone!

"Let the books we have already bequeathed be our gravestones, should your anger at our silence smite us a second death. But I too refuse to say anything new - if our audience in daylight life heeded not our words, then what use now to conjure new prose, or to do battle with words for an audience of one, and an alien at that. Command, ask, beg if you will of us words, but if in life we were not prophets worthy of being heard, then why would we wordsmith now, risen from the dead, for now we are comforted in our next life - leave us be, and let those who did not heed us live in agony.

"We two are of one mind - let our mouths be of stone, forever set, let our tongues be like rock, immovable, let us be exactly as we are now embodied, forever stuck, for we have spilt ink and blood enough. Ask of us another task, but not the alchemy of words, for there are already much too much of these.

"And let me tell you a truism, alien to your ears, Ajami, that though to life stone you bring, know that He who alone is Master, He alone can call forth something from nothing, and He alone can raise children from stones. You are not our master, nor our father – we owe nothing to you! Being mere playthings, we deny you even this enjoyment. Hear us well, we defy you, and your play.

"From us nothing will you receive, and if this angers you, then it is your powerlessness you truly rage against, but if you were truly powerful, from this nothing you could create something. Greater men than us tried to name that which was nameless, call into life that which could not stir nor breathe, and these died, as indeed we did, all in vain, to bring life from rock, the self-same rock, that the waves of your anger now crash against.

"Truly, Ajami, wisdom lies not in the clever flight of words. Accept what you dread to be revealed, and you will straightaway learn the truth: nothing comes from nothing and nothing will remain."

But it is no use, the demon is already distracted. Ajami recalls a corner, elsewhere in the Rose City, for his attention is one that is easily frustrated, and quickly drawn away. Not for him argument in this the hour of his play. Seeing no duel between these poets, only stubbornness, for which his indulgence is little, he dreams instead of a contest between singers.

"Then of nothing, let something come, for none will defy the hour's play due me!" And with a click of his neck, Ajami, the Goat, and the Nose stand before the Diminutive Chanson and the Bard of Three Muses. The former already met, wipes his stone fingers with a white kerchief, the latter, a chimaera of stone, has five eyes pouring melancholy, sorrow, and loss, the last two are grief and love battling for a consensus denied by a wall of nose.

"Now behold, you Goat and you Nose, if wordsmiths you both are, but nothing birth will you, then instead judges be in this contest. Speak not ill, but quickly when called upon, armed with history, let us together sit. If in agreement, then assent!" The stone necks creak agreement to their new role. "Then in place of duel between wordsmith poets, instead a competition of song, for we shall now ask, who is the greatest voice that these mountains ever echoed down into the valleys of their birth.

"For subject of song, let also introspection serve, now let us call you first, Chanson, and sing a little of thy journey to the Godless Hour."

The Diminutive Chanson rises and releases the kerchief from the grasp of his right hand, and clasps it instead in his left, and with the now free hand, he feigns a paintbrush.

With words he paints his story:

"Let me tell of a time that once was, but once was not; in alien land, ancestors roamed in lands of green on coasts far from home. Gifted with tongue, and versed in song, I sung such sweet things that all who heard were as one in their rapture, and in my native land, I was named 'favoured son' but it was birdsong I sung, not my native tongue, and though beneath the shade of trees the sparrow's song is sweet, it is on mountain peaks that the crane finds his sanctuary, his home, and in native tongue, there speaks.

"Tell me now, if you can, what makes a man a native son of this sweet land? Is it words? A love? Or deeds? Which of these tells '*he is of us, he is one of our number*'? Was I any less in life for not being *here*? Would I have homeland better served dancing in the old-fashioned way, the way my grandparents used to? Am I less a native son for being of guitars and not kemanchas? Answer me if you can, what makes a man of here? Give me answers and I will laugh at all you comedians, for what you lay at my feet - and watch as I transform before your eyes from alien to native, and back once more. For none can answer my question: what makes this, this, and that, that.

"Of this I am sure, one life is given, one life is lived, one life ends, and from this certainty we take one lesson: that life must go on. And what does life consist of, but learning to leave the table when love is no longer being served, and in leaving, pocketing one's pride, telling yourself all the time that you remain able to take leave of home without saying a word, to be taken a long, long way from here, from home - and there where you arrive, you will be something else, a curiosity before all eyes - neither this nor that, a crow amongst peacocks, and a peacock amongst crows, always a bird migrating, in search of nesting and feeding grounds, never able to rest, but knowing one life has been given, one life was lived, and one life ended, that life can go on.

"This is my birdsong, not lament, mind. Listen well, that no hint of regret imbues my melody, just the musings of a lifetime lived knowing two loves at once, but not knowing which to kiss first. But let me finish by speaking of the love, the first love of life, 'She'! She is the bosom of my birth, my mother tongue. She may be a hundred different things, measured in a hundred different ways, spoken of in a hundred different tongues, by a hundred different people, but the meaning of my life is She."

With that, the Chanson wipes his hands clean of fictitious paint, washes, and packs away his brushes, before settling himself back down to the rapturous applause that gurgles from the throat of Ajami, whose yelps of "Encore! Encore" are at once both mocking and lauding as though an audience of thousands is present, rather than a judgement of two.

"Now for the turn of the Bard of Three Muses..." says Ajami, grinning to the other combatant.

The Bard of Three Muses is a visage of terrible romanticism. Without his body, his work is less musical, and the half-closed eyes of his face accuse him of being a dreamer. His neck is craned taut, his lips pursed, seem to tremble mournfully; a crown of windswept hair speaks of a man defiantly turning his back to the West of the Chanson, and instead, allowing the violent Eastern wind to blow through him, blowing away his body, his work, and promising instead a babbling howl of oriental tongues to take their place.

And yet, tortured as he is, beside him three veiled muses with equine necks bow in supplication before him like congregants before an altar; the whispers of his silent lips are an incense to them, and even in this Godless Hour, perhaps here an old deity finds himself for a new age.

"Come forth and sing us a tune of yore, hunter of words, lord of song. Do battle with the Chanson and let us assembled judge who is the better, but let us improve our audience with a greater company!

"Come forth, the Fool, the Pro, and the Coward, and sit in attendance once more in the Caucasus. You too The Men who are engaged in halting walk. Come hither, you forgotten conspiracy of Abovyan Street, and take here new seats. Come now five men with broken noses and cloth caps led by one with thick hands and a round belly, behind whom is a fool with a cloak upon his head.

"Come, Albany and Cornwall, come, Burgundy and Lear with his Fool in his train, come, you men, Antonio and Bassanio, Gratiano, and Lorenzo, come, you Falstaff, Shylock, and Bottom - come, you trio, and you conspiracy, you camaraderie, come you all, welcome and join! The troll-like men of Abovyan, and the trio from the Caucasus, and with them The Men of Sayat Nova all gather and assemble themselves at the base of the Bard of Three Muses, a willing audience of tricksters, gourmands, lads and louts, bemused to live again, bemused to be called to spectate.

"Now Bard of Three Muses, begin!" commands Ajami.

The Bard's eyes open to reveal pupil-less rocks for eyes, rounded beneath their carved lids. He begins his song in weeping tones:

"In the whole breadth of the world no greater fruit did God give than the pomegranate.

"Its skin, when torn, weeps blood; when freshly cut, it lies sacrificed upon tabletop, an offering for the tabernacle.

"If too fat, and left to ripen on the branch, it bows earthwards, and falls, splitting open, its juice weeps forth as tears and stains the ground red. The branch whence it came holds aloof its arms, heavenwards, mourning.

"If plucked and uneaten, its flesh shrivels inwards and contracts tautly like weathered skin drying, until the pips alone remain to rattle like the creaking bones of the aged.

"Three muses, here beside me sit, three pomegranates I steal from paradise for them, but not to eat, but by which to learn.

"Let one know the flesh in murderous curiosity; she wounded me.

"Let one know the tears of the fallen fruit as they stain the ground; she broke me.

"And let the third know the fruit withered in her care, giving no flesh, no juice, and no seeds; she refused me.

"Blot out the vine, and forget any sweetness that honey may bring. Of rosewater, and mastic, coffee and all scents oriental exotic – let none come forth.

"For me the pomegranate is the whole world, each seed a promise of a new world. If offered not to the altar that is the lips of man, and his mouth a portal to God knows not its taste, if instead left to the soil, and not for man his appetite sate, what great forests may come of sweet ruddy trees and their ruby fruits which cling defiantly to the rocks, what stubborn greenery in groves flecked with red will prevail.

"Yes, the world is large, this is a truth, but so too is it true that each man is a pomegranate given, for an altar to place upon, but I, reckless wretch, gave mine to love, and the love of one – who ate her fill of my humble offering, for she tore apart my pomegranate, rent its skin like worn-out garb, and gorged herself upon its flesh. She made delicacy of what should be eaten delicately, for in each seed was the promise of a poem, a line of song, as yet to be sung, but she cracked the pip between her teeth, destroying the promise of a new life, and let the juice flow through her mouth to whet her tongue. Yet despite what even I brought her, I, Adam reversed, she could not eat her fill of my words offered either in native or alien tongue.

"And when my words did fail, when Armenian and Georgian had in their full measure run their course, I composed and wrote in Azeri, in distant Persian too, words I sung. Yet even this babel of song and prose, poetry and verbose, towering heavenward in climbing praise, was not enough to sate, and she, still not filled, looked at the husk that was me in my remnant, nothing more than a carcass to rot and be forgotten as just another foolish one.

"This chanson bemoans his tired past – he is but a little bird of two lands, flitting, forever on the wing. I, broken hearted, wandered the world, for a homeland, I had not even one! He writes and sings in Frankish tongue, and speaks of trees beneath which to hear birdsong, not a lonely exile his.

"No shelter did I find under trees, only in the sallow inwards of monasteries did respite find me worthy.

"Not for me, dreary assembled, the sparrow's chirp or call of the crane. No! Instead, the nightingale cooed to me, and I followed when called, and cast aside my longings and versed song. I departed the earthly land and to heaven turned my gaze, to the Lord above I turned my song.

"And as with now, words of stone filled my mouth till my lips could no longer part, and my tongue had no space to move – hands that once plucked at play or dragged pen across parchment lay firmly set in prayerful place, till lofty thoughts of God lifted my head from the earthly desires my captive body still sought.

"So that when the end day came, when that Persian Shah by sword cleft my head from my neck and firmly did part bard from body, he only confirmed by violence a parting already agreed by head and heart.

"What remained of the pomegranate? It withered on the branch. Nought came forth. Nothing stained the soil red. No seeds remained in this husk to take a root. Instead of a forest, a grove – even a single tree – here instead I am, beheaded as on my passing day.

"What I was, I am now set in stone, a memory of the past. My words barely parting my lips whisper to the sideways glance, of these three muses, forever walking away. Passer-by in life, here I lie, doomed to forever be unknown."

With this the Bard of Three Muses ends his offering and closes his eyes once more, and though the stone monk still moves with subdued breath, it is as though the Godless Hour has ended its patience with him.

The three muses weep, ogled each in turn by the Fool, the Coward, and the Pro, whilst the Conspiracy of Abovyan Street, Lear and his attendees break into applause, chanting in unison: "Nothing comes from nothing"; meanwhile, The Men seek to console, but theirs is a rabble of noise, and all are soon silenced.

"Now," says Ajami the Judger, turning to the Goatlike One and the Torso-less Nose alike, "two great singers you have heard on their native soil - tell me which is the greater? Which is the combatant better? First you, Great Nose, sneeze a little more your thoughts that we might bless you."

The Nose rocks upon his pedestal as though in agonised thought as to whom to declare for, then he turns to the assembly and says:

"To me the victor must be the Bard. My reasons are threefold.

"Firstly, that his name, the hunter of words, is true, for though alien words litter his diction, so too did his pen draw out sun sweet words under which to bask.

"Secondly, though his roaming is of heart alone, body and mind took him across the East, and yet still in death throes, he found himself martyred in the land of Nairi.

"Thirdly, finally, he, like me, is not as he once was, for both of us now stand bodiless for eternity, or at least until some new would-be conqueror comes to erase this land once more, and we heads together must stick, for two are better than one, but also less those with limbs should wonder why our guises alone, and not our bodies in total, are enough to speak of us."

To this reasoning Ajami laughs knowingly and accepts the Nose's judgement. "Now you, Old Goat, bleat some, and baa, baa, baa if you will, but know that night is not endless, so speak little, and in little say much, lest your judgement be faulted."

The Goat is swift in judgement:

"To me the clear winner is the Chanson. The world is large, and the children of this land lie scattered within, without, with root, or withered.

"Not their fault the unkindness of history's tread and the world's injustice - not all who are scattered can be ingathered, but if in their heart a native drum still beats and eyes do not askance gaze, instead, they still look upon the homeland and to all who listen tell the story with the familiar breath, 'I lived to tell the tale…' then this to me is the greater son, for it is not a lament for what was lost he sings, but defiantly alive, declaring to the world, see what of one scattered seed came, what a tree, and from it, what a fruit, now think what more might have come were it not for the bitter harvest from which this one fruit alone fell, and fell not far.

"Sure, the whole world is contained in a pomegranate, but out it bursts forth, and a seed that took root in foreign land, but grew towards the sunlight of its long-lost land triumphs in song over the traveller whose road of departure began not at the loss of home, but at heartbreak."

At the Goat's bleat's end, Ajami the Trickster laughs and claps his hands ecstatically so that a thunder clap breaks the silence of the otherwise weather-less sky, and not to be outdone, a lightning flash rents the darkness in two to signal a natural law still present, and that even the Godless Hour will close.

"How marvellous! How brilliant! How ever to be expected – friendship in deadlock drowned, no consensus to be had here. Let us bring forth a final judge. May he complete our panel and let us agree that before sunrise his shall be the deciding vote."

From the darkness emerges the Oaken Priest, his like so many eyes broken into a permanent glaze. He shuffles along in muffled footsteps, not for him the Godless Hour, no desire had he to be woken, but now at Ajami's command he too takes his place between the Goat and the Nose and though not present at the contest, his ears have heard much in the solitude of his oaken throne where he once sat alone.

"Now Oaken Priest, we are of one mind agreed that yours shall be the judgement of Paris, the deciding vote is yours to cast. Speak little mind, for the hours of each

The Ashoughs

minute in the Godless Hours gasp swiftly and as in life, no long sermon is called for here."

The Oaken Priest rests himself upon a stump, and hands rest upon his lap, his doe eyes forever blankly stare as though blind to the others there assembled. It is as though he sees things unseen, even in this time of unseeing where an hour is comprised of many hours.

Slowly, he creaks into homily:

"Judge not lest ye be judged, scripture teaches us, and yet you call upon a man of the cloth to preside. What can I say that poets and troubadours have not in the traffic of their tongues already offered? I rent my tear-stained garb in protest at the task you set – but who am I to judge?

"In life I was worth less than nought, one task alone is my life's cause that what the ear hears, the hand transcribes in notation. Truly, I was a scribe, and no musician; a note-taker of unfortunates is all, one who rendered life to the forgotten, the half-forgotten, the doomed to be further forgotten. I was a creator, only in part. Even the stonemason who called me forth from stone could not create the stone, so I too, transcribed, and brought forth music from mouths to parchment, a Moses before the burning bush, holding God's tablets before the nation assembled. What more than that did I create, that I might be said to be a master of anything?

"What is so great that I might be brought here, and here to hear, and to judge whose is the best song - if this you press me upon, then I respond, judge not lest ye be judged.

"These brothers of mine in song are wordsmiths both, I but a scholar, a supplicant at the hem of music's skirt, and there, in my place once upon a time, I did not judge what was worthy of record, only concluding that everything deserved to be recorded. My only choice, to decide what is to be saved, and now in death, in a hell I reside, for locked in my head, for me alone to listen, in ever repeating loop, all that I found not the time to transcribe, all that will remain forever dead, all an anthem to those moments when I said enough for one evening and lay my pen to rest. These lost songs are now demons that prick and burn me, so many deceased thoughts. They are lost souls that torment my conscience; I know no peace.

"So, let it be enough for this night, and all nights, that song exists, that a people exists to sing these songs, a people exists to hear the singing of these songs. For let me say once more: I will not judge who is to be favoured son, but will only delight in his song."

Ajami the Irritable jumps into mid-air, and therein lingers with flailing arms - before calming, he bellows hoarsely:

"Then be damned all of you! All you men of words! All you men of song - poets and minstrels alike, and you most of all, cloth-garbed one - you who will not parley in prose, and you who will not judge, damn you!

"You who sing, a curse upon you, be as cheap as birdsong, for drunken revelries and mumbled half-remembered recitals. You ingrates, you peddlers of nothing, who will not play, truly you deserve these rock pedestals you sit upon; they are truly your gravestones. If you will not play my games, then I who gave you rock-borne life, say to bed with you each one, to bed with you all! Wake not again, and return to bed, to be passed by and forgotten!

"The crowns I would have given you this night, not to be - be satisfied instead with the floral wreaths of whatever poor romantic fool remembered whatever anniversary that brings them to pray ofference at your stone feet. Better the baying of dogs than the swansong of this folly. I could have made bread from you rocks, from you, food for your people! Instead, good night! Let the people starve on your words, nothing that they are, from nothing come forth nothing! Be an intimate for the people of this valley."

With that Ajami the Angered dismisses them all, and they each return to his shaded, birdshit-ridden corner of the city.

Come back the baying packs of dogs to Ajami's whistle, and where music had filled the silence, now only the howls and yelps of the orphan hounds play accompaniment to the Godless Hour.

This too is soon drowned out by the clash of thunderous gallops as the Four Horsemen of Yerevan awake, and the Godless Hour draws on calling Ajami the Infantile to play his games elsewhere.

IV

The Horsemen

"...and asked him what country this was. He replied that it was Armenia. Then they asked him for whom the horses were being kept, and he said that they were a tribute paid to the King."

—Xenophon

A great beast of a horse, Dzhalali, makes an entrance in galloping roar and in so doing tears through the streets of Yerevan. His flowing mane is a crest of flamelike tongues, and it frames a wide-eyed gaze which in turn crowns flaring nostrils almost bursting open so maddeningly wide are they. A foaming muzzle speckles the cobblestones with spittle that falls like manna, though there are no Israelites to partake.

Wherever Dzhalali's hooves crash down in stampede, sparks fly. Wherever he charges, stones quake.

Wherever he progresses, is briefly his conquest.

No simple stallion this steed, not a creature to stable, instead a charge of Helios has broken free from his yoke hitherto chained, and a dim sun charges the lengths of Yerevan's thoroughfares mocking the city with a false dawn.

Atop Dzhalali's back sits not a giant; instead, standing in the stirrups and wielding a sword of flashing greatness, a blade of nothing less than pure lightning, is a champion of yore.

He is a myth.

No freedom fighter this giant. No man of honour, nor one belonging to a cause. He will not command men atop horseback, but instead, loathe to arrogantly spill the blood of his enemies' footmen in wanton slaughter, for such rank and file are but chaff to his blade, would see it right to instead challenge the enemy chieftain to single combat and thereby spare so many widows their tears through a single man's feat of arms.

He is a fossil, of a fiction time, when the greats hid not behind strategy, nor behind the ranks of men- doomed-to-be-fodder, but of that time from yesteryear when the bravery of one triumphed the multitudes of the many. Those whose numbers were dissolved in unjust conquest, those who in their namelessness were unenumerable, those were all who fell littered beneath his blade, there to be forgotten, save that his name, in being remembered served them as their gravestone, and thereby, such innumerable nameless were saved by memory.

He is of the time when heroes were worthy of song, and such songs sired legends. That distant time, when the wits of so many kings crumbled before the bravery of so very few.

Here rides the Daredevil of Sassun - with spark flecking horse's hooves beneath him and lightning-like sword above him, he brings not war, but a light, an illumination to his progress as he races around the great circular square of the Rose City. He is the foreshadower, rendering the square tonight, a hippodrome.

He is a light to that truth so easily hidden in the shadows that myths should spill ink not blood.

He is a myth who should have stayed in his pages, rather than set an impossible example cited by would-be sages.

Not for long alone does the Daredevil charge in his circuit, for soon, this Myth is joined by the Legend. Now comes hither the tragic plumed helm of that son of Mamikon. His sword is held aloft, but shield-less; his free hand is outstretched, beckoning forth a sally from those who are wedded to the last stand, or commanding a rout to rally, only the onlooker can decide which is author to this his final charge.

He is at once both the victor and the defeated, doomed to play both parts in the tireless theatre that is history's debate.

He alone knows that a people who will fall, that they might stand again, only to fall once more, are never the defeated for they can never be vanquished.

He rides upon a Grecian steed that flails dust in its wake, and with each galloping stride makes short work of miles.

Ajami narrates this pilgrim's progress, so overcome is the demon by the sight of this Legend:

"Come, you Hector, son of Ilium whose line fails, yet name lives on! Come, you fallen Trojan, and consider that had you lived, your tragedy would not compare to this plumed brave. To this Persian-bane, whom, like you, loyal to a fault, was for his loyalty slain. For just as your cause did Greek duplicity greet after the death your honour did make you meet, and thereby your people's fate was sealed, come now and reflect in this mirror, here is your equal revealed.

"Come now, Leonidas, you laconic king, lord of quick quip and quicker blow. You too knew the might of hordes in service to Persian excess, alas too well! And just as you with sword raised defiantly knew the enemy would overcome however high the wall was made of stacked Spartan dead, you still swore to breathe your last tired breath before Shah's sheer numbers overwhelmed; here is the same man who swore death and freedom, your own battle cry, he, like you when facing tyranny, knew it was only to die.

"Come, Leonidas, and meet your successor who followed your path of folly.

"Marvel, is he not as noble? Is he not as hopeful? Does he, not unlike you, take the fight to his enemy, knowing too that numbers, not just cause, will prevail?

"Look too, all you Bogatyr and Braves, Sarmatians and Scythians, Cossacks, Kazakhs, Huns! All you men of horseback who rode to meet Persia, and flew from their parting short. Look here, Idanthyrsus, you horse-lord of Scythia, Psammeticus, you final Pharaoh. Come too, Croesus of Lydia, who happy as you were, mourned that your wealth could save you not.

"Come, all you failed kings and fallen heroes, all you Greeks and Romans who fought the might of Persia, and read, by dawn of Persian light, the writing on the wall, and knew that the days before you were counted, drawn, and measured, just like old Belshazzar, the first of your number to fall.

"See now here your kinsman in failed venture, call him brother, here is he, the Mamikon! He, who like you took on Persia knowing the outcome was foregone! He, who like you knew that death, if knowingly embraced, is with eternal life blessed, though on the list of Persian conquest his entry remains anonymous.

"But had he heeded the lessons your examples taught, and by them avail, well would he have learnt that one does not stand before Iran and win; that only those who march to Fars and vanquish shah therein, prevail. But since that Macedonian of centuries past, not one has been born who could make ease of such a task.

"See him, all you brothers-in-arms who fell before Persian sword, Persian lance, Persian bow, and bring him into your fraternity, call him brother in blood as he too takes his place in the Godless Hour's unending, unwinnable race.

"See him and marvel, for no army follows him, no restless nomad host, no chariots of the Nile race, no three hundred in his guard, and no history book contains an etching of his face."

And having rhapsodised the entry of the Legend, Ajami pauses his merriment to sombrely applaud.

Not for mockery this one rock rendered alive.

To this two, comes a third: the Fedayi.

This one's back was not made to prostrate itself before a scimitar, trembling in imitation of its cruel curve. He is all rippling muscle and overblown machismo. Moustache-donning and bare-chested he trails a Bulgarian cape behind him whilst above his head a sword is raised heavenwards, its pommel and blade conspiring to form a cross, but not one he will bear, save as arms to further his cause.

His cape, a cassock, caught in the wind of the charge, his blade, the holy cross, this is a warrior monk avowed to the cause, and just as his banner calls forth the brave, from his chest he bellows: "Freedom!" and by feat of arms he promises to save them.

No battalion of soldiers will ever be his to lead, but motley braves rally to his call. Even though they know that he too is doomed to defeat, they follow him, one and all. From peasant-born sons, and broken men, outcasts all, he rallied the dispersed and forged a band of sworn brothers, who in oath, pledged to wed liberty, and in that bride's bosom, the only lovers embrace worthy to know, found the pregnant promise of a new life: freedom, alas, was stillborn.

His call, still, is: "Rally!" and they obey like the faithful attending communion.

No single combat does he offer, no defiant charge of one against the many, he too is destined to find the tragedy of failed cause, the salt of so many ancestors' supper.

No one will face him alone, and no great conquering army will march to meet him. He is the one undefeated in battle, but doomed to be defeated by war.

"Rally!" and he rides to the hippodrome of the Rose City's centre atop his two steeds. For so great is the urgency of his task that he has dispensed with chariot, thrown away the yoke that binds, and because his resolved stride will outdo the gallop of any single horse, only two can outpace him, and they cajole him to ride their bare backs, a conjoined saddle - this then becomes the manner of his entry.

No great poem for him. No incense to be burnt either. Only songs and toasts will tell of him, though he asked in life for less words, and to spill blood, not spill drink instead.

Behold this freedom fighter who turned mountain redoubts into eyries and therein eagle-eyed, spied a land to be quenched of blood, not drenched thereof.

Behold you freedom fighters now, the great Fedayi! And all those who turned to ploughing, having smelt their swords, all you Irish and Gibrans, here is your hero! He who descended from mountain peaks to liberate the plains fastness, he who answered your prayers and descended, whilst Saint Michael with his angelic hosts met your prayers with silence and remained ascended.

Not born to leadership, but thrust upon him, he charges beside the Myth and the Legend and in his grandsires' shadows seeks to correct their historic mistakes. Too many vainglorious moments have left his tribe in servitude, he mutters, no honour, nor pitched battle, no justice will atone for the romance they have written into their defeats. Instead the rallying call of freedom still echoing from childish stories and church sermons must now be heard as a clarion call to arms, this is his vow. How sweet its sound when uttered by his stony lips, how it first commands the ears of men and then commands their hearts.

Behold here is he whose cries fell on deaf ears, those self-same whose hearts were broken.

Last to the race comes the Marshall of Karabagh. He of no drawn sword. No muscular girth, nor windswept hair, there is nothing remarkable about the horse that bears him other than that it trots in assuredness, rather than gallop in urgency, or stampede in alarm.

The Marshall is broad-shouldered confidence conveyed upon horseback. He needs no myths, no legends, no tall folk tales to be told. His is a record captured in the hoard of medals that weighs upon his chest: circled stars for valour, triangles within squares for bravery, angles and edges all, an array of medals so dense, they make a chainmail of sorts.

And just as his chest serves only as display, so too those same broad shoulders play host to a drawn cape as though daring the wind to make it flutter.

Here rides a martial spirit whose love of war would make these other horsemen blush. No longer the youth

The Four Horsemen

who dreamt of liberating homelands and drawing new lines on maps to say here be us, and there be them, no! This is Ares! This is Mars! This is Vahagn – a god of war!

He sees only the enemy, and thereby his myopia, something that exists only to be destroyed. He is strategy, for whom armies offer only challenge. War is his calling, his passion, his muse. He talks of forts, not homes, and Valkyries, not wives. The din of battle is the only lullaby he knows, and its sound soothes him better than any opera.

He is fury, for whom borders are meaningless lines, dashes on a map to be overcome, and thereafter, reassembled into pointing arrows to thrust at the enemy whoever he be. For this hero has no nemesis – for once the

Turk was this role, only for the Hun to have taken his place.

Son of liberty? Son of *patrie*?

Or just sporting for a fight?

Look now, all you Persians, Zhukovs, Romans, and Germans, here is your contemporary, no less worthy of song for having come from some mountainous corner that history decreed should otherwise be forgotten. No Cossacks at Poltava, no knights, no Agincourt, not for him Yankees and Gettysburg, or Panzers and Stalingrad, no, he sees no victory as conclusion. He spoils for no greater cause than the next fight, and onward to the next victory, and thereafter further victories in wars as yet unknown.

Who will recall this formidable in history, whose name alone belies the ends of the earth? What grandiose great his victory flag unfurled heralds?

Here is our god of war, a general red, no old schoolbook hero, dusty epic, or ill-recalled legend. He is not doomed to fall, not doomed to see his homeland burn, no, here be a warrior to command warriors! He sees no nation, only a band of brothers loyal in their marching orders, loyal in never asking "why?" For whoever sheds their blood unerringly and by his command, is his brother, more so than any native son born to his neighbour in those valleys far from the campaign trail upon which he marches forward with a new name: Augustine, Alexandrine, Unknown. He too takes his place in the cavalcade that rides through the great square, tonight rendered hippodrome.

The four riders of the night race their steeds in magnificent succession, alternating leads as each one in turn speaks.

The first to ride forth and take the lead is the Myth atop his impossible steed. He races ahead of the others in the hippodrome and sets the race:

Sassun in Vaspurakan, now forever lost,
Was my distant home
Though throughout the highland mountains
My adventures beckoned I roam.
Of royal line I claim descent,
Whilst my actions so great, were heavenly ascent.
Far did I rove on quests many,
Great were the battles against mine enemy.
Mher my father and Dzhalali my steed
My birthright, both, also ordained my deeds.

Not for me the foreign milk of Mosul, never
Nor the miserable exile of distant Misr.
Instead on native honey, native butter, native wine, was I weened
And on native food a longing did I concede
For in the court of the king of Mosul
Did my years ripen and I came of age,
And in this foreign land I conceived such thoughts
To right my homeland's ill-fate was all I sought.
This great cause my taskmaster did become
I set myself to fight until this deed was done!

So great my voice that the wild beasts did concede
Of a herdsman were they in need.
When I tired of herding to hunting I took,
Replacing with bow and arrows, my shepherd's crook.
And thus armed I did clear the native lands
Of fell beast, marauder, and robber bands.
Where once there was a desolate waste

A great monastery did I erect in haste
To tempt the wrath of the lord of Mosul
And fight that tyranny, and vanquish all evil.

"Withdraw from Armenia, oh alien one!"
I roared as sabres and armour glittered in the sun
I slew his braves who dared defy my command
Those who deemed it fit to spoil Sassun's land.
But this countless slaughter I could not tolerate.
For the blood that was spilt would not abate
So, when Mosul's great king emerged at the head of his host
He called to me in vainglorious boast
He meant to end me, my like, exile, and ravage my land,
All I know to fire, and defile, if I should not kiss his hand.

But I being Sassun born, was deaf to his call
And met his chattering with a lion's roar.
Not of me will they say courage faltered,
Instead they will sing praises of the man assured
I who am courage born and therein wrought
Was of mind resolved and set forth
Not to have men in vast numbers die in vain,
But to challenge the king in single combat
By one man's feat alone prove that
Sassun, her sons and plains, could breathe free, again.

Victory was brief how well known a refrain
Aged did I grow and when youth was no more
Took I my leave through father Mher's door.
Know this though, when the hour doth come
When so terrible is the fate that we are nearly done
Then will I return from whence I did depart
Fear not aslumbered, keep me in your heart
And know that though all seems it cannot be worse
Your Son of Sassun has not yet returned home
Therefore, the greatest of trials is yet unknown.

The Myth having finished is swiftly overtaken in the Godless Hour's race by the Legend, who, turning back to look upon his predecessor, rebukes him thusly:

"You talk in praise of deeds done half done - who is to say if they ever were?! Now let me take my turn as leader of the charge." And in turn he begins his own poetic soliloquy:

Know ye not of conflict, other than by feat of arms?
Of Christian faith duty bound to alms and psalms,
I speak, of its conflict with my royal service,
Which decreed despatch forth to Asian wastes furthest;
There by Shah's fitful command I slew the vile Hun,
And when to Caesar such feats were rendered done,
I was whence recalled by Persian king to court
With those noble spirits with whom battles fought.

There called upon to forswear the faith,
To betray to conceit what was conceived by ancestors late;
We took our leave, together to return home,
Resolved to save our people's souls and forsake our own.
For to save the people further visit by tragedy
I, and my brothers, foreswore the faith and bent the knee.
Better this sleight of honour thought us to conspire,
Than see Persian might turn our land into a mire!
What loss is one soul to eternal damnation?
Better that be lost than nation know desolation!

Denouncing my faith, pleading loyalty to the Shah,
Home I returned turning thought to exile far;
To take leave of all I know and leave native abode
Thereby abate dishonour and salve my forebode.
Whilst thusly serving the people vested as my charge

News soon reached of rebellion at large.
Oh, sweet fatherland oathbound to protect
You chose my error to correct.

I ask you, how does one serve such a people
Who would rather don the martyr's mantle?
Those self-same rendered conquerors' fodder
Who would rather all die than one soul falter?
How does one save such a people as thee?
Who when told to submit and bend the knee
Bare their necks and plead: Cut here instead!
"Leave us our faith, send us to our deaths!"

It was with pride and vows and half-berating that
I took up leadership of Armenia's doomed covenant.
My king-less people intoned: "Lead us to victory, or death
Lead us to martyrdom, or saintly example set!"
How does one reason with a single-minded voice?
Truly there is no hope for those who chose no choice!
When they asked I lead them forth to their destruction
I prayed: "God forgive Armenia's bloody ablution."

I tell you they are a stubborn people who will never submit
Forsooth they will never dare perish for the debt
That their God owes them in their steadfast defiance
Of all those conquerors' swords they met with prayer's reliance,
But truly they had before them easier paths to tread,
Had they but chosen yielding roads instead
But where the people wish to go, I will lead them
Even if so doing serves our nobility's deletion.

I rode our numbers out to that cursed Avarayr,
There to irrigate with blood that field dire.
Outnumbered, outmanned, doomed, outdone;
There we gathered in ranks of steel: father stood beside son
We all were ready to clash our mettle and fate meet
In the presence of our enemies, martyrdom greet.

Though we were a merry band of brothers, we few
God had arrayed Persia against us, the odds we knew.

Before the enemy I saw the truth of Greeks' schooling
For though we fought on the morrow it was evening
So great were the arrows Persia let fly
The sun itself was blotted out from the sky.
Vast in number were the Shah's armies ranked deep
Mark it no Ancient lie that the king that day did weep.
Persia ruled one hundred realms, scripture teaches
But what doth it profit the lost soul, it also preaches.

Thus, we assembled a company of rocks before Persian tide
We stood before this empire, resolute never to hide
Knowing too well the crashing waves would not tire
When all here were drowned our lands would afire
What hope we, when once three hundred fell?
On eve of battle my mind on such thoughts did dwell:
Ready to be martyred for faith, stubborn necked, doomed to die
All so they could say we kept the truth and countenanced no lie.

You horseman are only a bedtime's tale
A children's delight, but a meaningless fable.
I, however, am a rougher cut, for I am legend
I lead the people in pitched battle to teach them lesson
To dissuade them of stories and fabulous grandiosities
And hope that they disregard storytellers' fantasies.
Instead herein these books read the truth, and contented be,
That to a nation born is he who knows death embraced is immortality!

As the Legend brings his soliloquy to a close, his steed tires and falls into a slower paced trot, before being in turn overtaken. Now is the turn of the Fedayi to gallop in metre:

Truly of such great things do you both speak
That my rock heart turns once more to beating flesh

And pumping blood renders me no more weak
For an evening again I am with life blessed.
In the cradle was I nursed on such stories;
Of heroes, battles, and adventures told;
That yesteryear was filled with past glories,
Whilst priests' sermons spoke of saints of old.

It was of you Legend, that I partook communion.
For how could I hear of such valour
And remain a carpenter's apprentice, what delusion!
In church I heard no parables, nought of our saviour
That spoke of such a profession as true calling
For had I kept my father's trade and led life Nazarene
Then whenever you Legend I remembered, galling,
Would be the thought of what might have been.

I saw the cross, not for my back hewn from wood
But upright and turned upside down in the air
A symbol of might that would serve cause good
I decided to turn back to sword the ploughshare.
When in church I knelt in prayerful thought
In my mind's eye God revealed cross shaft as handle
Beyond that hilt, pommel, and blade He wrought
And forged a sword in the flicker of church candle.

Where others saw their homeland a desolation
God ordained that I saw what others were blind to see
Visions from angels filled my dreams with liberation
And in waking hours I prayed louder than mullah's cry: liberty!
Were I born in such days of yore when champions took to field
Or men arrayed in decimated ranks for desperate last stand
Then I whose heart is a lion's roar would never yield
But fight the good fight till we were cut down to last man!

Such days as your myths and legends are in found
Are behind us now like so many lost lands
Best kept wrapped away in half-forgotten books

And passed between scholars' hands
Pack up your stories and leave them to nursemaids
Our people called for a new hero, a new leader
Whose rallying cry was a comfort declaring: "You are saved!"
Rather than priests and scholars' offerings meagre.

In my day the enemy was not in some far capital
Not some oriental despot of foreign land distant
Who marched and plundered like some ravened animal.
No! The enemy was in our midst and about us, constant
And our people what had become their fate?
Downtrodden and broken, a fallen hovel-living race
Whose paltry tributes, the ravenous, could not be sate
No more sword wielding, shield bearing, nor cavalry charging at pace.

Now to me and my band fell the task to rally our people all
And from the mountaintops high we thundered a cry
"To arms, dear brothers, leave farms, dear brothers, heed this call!
God and foreigners, dear brothers, promise hope, dear brothers, but they lie!"
Did they answer the call of Sassun? No, in fields they stayed and ploughed.
You, oh Myth, hidden in mystical cliff, door closed, never rode!
Did they recall their saintly legends? No, in churches they offered prayers less loud.
You too, oh Legend, in heaven dwelling when incense was burning, never roused!

There can be no doubt that mine was a cause lost
That liberty pursued was a bride sought in vain
That Armenia's redemption had too high a cost
Misery and suffering is our repeated refrain
Mine eyes destined not to see a homeland free

Instead saw Armenia bleed men, lose ground, once more
Till what was left clung to rocks, an eagle's eyrie
Of that once upon time land, what remained so small.

Of myths and legends, we have spent this eve in speak
While our people went on dreaming, forever asleep
Stories only piecemeal true became our daily bread
And for littering our land with tales not armies instead
To your number, I too join ranks, we three a trio:
The false myth, forgotten legend, and me, our last hero.

With the end of his rhyme, the Fedayi falls into equal pace with the Myth and the Legend. They ride in unison, and in their cantering the Marshall comes to the forefront of the race. Though the others sing in the lullabied tone of poetry, he takes his turn to speak prosaically:

"I heard your songs from my mother's lips as I played by her knee, you Myth.

"Whilst at sermons I paid little heed, but on the day of your feast, oh Legend, I sat bolt upright and paid attention; ready to march to war to avenge our fallen dead, deceased by Persian excess.

"At your grave I wept, Fedayi, I was once but an infantryman in your brigade, not much more, but far greater did I roam: not to fight distant shah in Persian redoubt, nor Red Sultan locked in his harem, nor Caliph in Baghdad, or misery from Misr or king of Mosul, all these distant despotisms that plagued our homeland with their carnal excesses and covetous eyes were by my day of weary agedness spent forces. Though I knew them well in my youth, they did not withstand the test of time, becoming footnotes over which historians scour and bleed ink, not for soldiers and blood to pour.

"In my youth I was a fiery patriot impassioned to join the liberation of my homeland, but as the blood cooled and dust settled, a nation stood in boundaries defined. No myths, no legends to my ears quickened, lies each of them - one and all. Only gunfire and sabre rattle, and the myriad cries of a thousand men called my attention as years did progress.

"True, not all were gathered, and lands remained in adulterous embrace, much was lost forever, but nonetheless there it stood, frail, but standing, risen again, this new foal on unsteady feet within the great herd of nations. And when on to steadier legs the foal clamoured, I found this foal a ready stallion, my mount, and rode him to face new generals on distant battlefields. For on war was I weaned on, and ever doomed to know, but not for me the taste of defeat, so on, to victory, forever, I go!

"For in these times where we are agreed there is no further need of tact, let me of truisms speak instead.

"Are we not agreed, too, that where hero's hopes, hero's skills, hero's last stands are made the stuff of legends, wet-nurses to new braves, we have succeeded in sending these poor deluded only to their graves? For truly all tonight assembled know that true love of liberty knows no fatherland, but is a cause in itself, a single banner to march under, a single drumbeat to march to, and what a poor call by comparison is the one for one's home's defence, when greater causes, with greater glory, call out for your share of endeavour in the great offensive!

"Thankful am I for example made of you Myth, you Legend, and you Hero, it was in your embrace I found home, and by your example set, cause. But in your roaming to Mosul, and back, or Persian capital, and back, to Macedonia, and back, it was all in the service of that whisper: 'home' – and how fickle a bride was she, forever ready, but unwilling, forever denying us the wedding night. 'No!' I said to that.

"I took my leave of this endless wedding feast that saw us forever celebrating chastity and never the nuptial night, and further I went, far from my native black garden, far off, to the ruins of those Goths and Huns, those Deutsches and Devils, with their Nietszches and Nazis, there, in the Wolf's Lair a new foe did I meet.

"Not for me a motley band to lead against overwhelming odds. No cavalry charge nor archers' flurried arrowed flight, but instead, tanks and mortars, and men of all nations marched under my command: Slavs and Turks, Tatars and Sarmatians! Men in their millions, an army whose numbers dwarfed the ghosts of our own past in their multitudes, thus did I lead in command, with which, did I conquer.

"I looked beyond my homeland for care and cause and for it, was I less a Mars? Or no equal of Napoleon? Did Hannibal in his elephantine feat surpass me? Or even Alexander, who wept for the moon? "None of these men could know the love of a cause beyond one's nose. For me, bloodshed washed away the memory of bloodshed: a baptism in each battle new.

"Truly we are a genius people, with no little measure of bravery, but note now well how you gallop in life but ever behind my sauntering trot, for truly brothers in arms, it is when we look out beyond our borders we excel, but obsessed to define them, we fall in droves, 'tis our lot. All too quickly we're ready to form part of a last charge, rather that, than of troubled history discharge!

"Come count now, brothers, of us there are only four, and heed me, heed my words, for they are not cheap, better we look outward than in, better on the offence, then defence, and better forwards to lands anew, lest we band of four in our number herald a fifth as due."

The Four Horsemen calm their race at the hippodrome, at such moment as the Godless Hour chants "end" will the winner be declared. However, as all are asleep, and already Ajami has taken leave of their company, the winner of this race will only be known to the jealous silence that is the only audience of the Godless Hour.

V.

The Bolsheviks

"And the ark rested in the seventh month, on the seventeenth day of the month, upon the mountains of Ararat."

—Genesis 8:4

Ulyanov stirs from his captivity.

Chained in some backstreet, he lies, there to be forgotten. His is a lonely grave.

Where once he stood proud, hand sweeping out to the beckoning future, now he lies forever horizontal, an embarrassing reminder of a bygone age.

Bound in chains, the archworker awakens.

He breaks free from his fetters, rouses himself up onto his feet, and like any infant, he takes his unknowing first steps. He is reborn. Where once begrudgingly revered, he is now a cursed name in this scrap of territory.

His raised eyebrow damns this nation, a pondering twist of his goatee breaks the dream of its freedom, and one scribble of his name scrawled on parchment seals its fate.

Ajami greets Ulyanov's awakening: "Spill ink, spill blood, spill words, Ulyanov, and see how they will all come, all those supplicants of yore to suckle once more at your side.

"Hark now, and look fast, Ulyanov, at how lonely is the company you keep this evening, how unready an audience it is you find to hear you.

"Let it not shock you.

"For you alone amongst the stoneworks hidden in this valley, were unloved. You were just another tyrant to a people already broken and so used to kowtowing to tyrants, that you, great would-be redeemer and saintliest saint, noticed not that they never accepted you. You misheard in their silence, agreement, when in fact, the better ear would have heard their truthful whisper: that they were tired of tyrants long before you came, you were just another.

"You were no deliverance to them. No salve nor saviour – just another padishah, dressed this time not in oriental garb, but in the raiment of a godless prophet, one whose temples were factories and whose incense was fumes. They knew you all too well, and that you were like any other. Something to endure for a time, but something that would not last the test of time.

"You are a perfect soothsayer for this Godless Hour: sing Ulyanov! Sing, and no music will play. Speak, Ulyanov! Speak, and see that no scribe will meet your words with frenzied jotting. Yesterday's man you are, and today's dawn has only fading memory of you, you who are last night's nightmare. Even the dogs will not now bay at your heels, for you offer not even a pedestal to piss against anymore. How lowly have you fallen, Ulyanov, where once nations gathered as one people to fly your bloody red banner, now all only see the verdancy of green dollar."

Ulyanov stands before his scion, that son of Shirvan, the Prophet Zartosht; all wispy haired and doleful eyed, a mournful face to be sure, he gives all his tears to the Caspian, and the Caspian consumes them with gluttonous waves.

"Greetings comrade," says Ulyanov.

"Greetings" comes the reply, and then silence fills the space between them somewhat disrespectfully. But the Godless Hour is not limitless and wants not for such pause's interruption of its mock symphony and so as both in life had much to say, so too now the words come gushing.

"What a paradise on earth we made," says Ulyanov, taken aback by all he sees.

The Prophet Zartosht laughs derisively at him. "Look on your works, mighty Ulyanov, and despair, for these…" and he sweeps his palm outwards, "these are not the fruits of our labours with leaky pens, we men of action, but rather the children of our most hated and detested enemy. Broken we are, our cause neither just, nor enviable is long spent, no sword will carry it, save to the wasteland, it is gone, never to rise again. We are relics. Think to why you are no longer raised atop your pedestal, but instead are a better-to-be-forgotten artefact exiled to a backstreet, there encased in iron bonds, and in a backyard dumped to rot beneath the elements. Now you are no longer a herald of a new red dawn, but instead an embarrassment to be done away with if only one knew how to."

Ulyanov looks askance into the unrelenting blackness of night. He has known exile before, but never like this, none so perfect and complete. The Prophet Zartosht is right. No more for him the sunlit steppe, nor the haloed Caucasus, instead, a dusty enclosure behind a forgotten sideroad of a sideroad, there, only for the rain to beat upon and the wind to chip away. What need does one have of hellfire if one is doomed to live as stone for all eternity and whose fate is to go from remembrance to dismemberment.

"But what of our dream to birth a new brotherhood of man, uniform, and all together equal, all of one dedicated opportunity and for it, in single-minded pursuit: I saw trains and factories, families and full bellies, wheat and steel and..."

"Stop!" says the Prophet Zartosht. "They did not want these things. 'Freedom!' they cried and their cry was heard.

"They are a stubborn people - they would rather eat their rocks than fill their bellies with bread! Better their sons and daughters wash up on distant shores and there find work than herein live, these people who know only what it is to disperse, what need do they have of land? What a hope, what a dream, is this land, where so much of what they call home is unredeemed - you thought Yerevan was ever enough? No, not enough for them! What of Van, and Cilicia, of Nakhichevan, of Karabagh!

They dreamt of bicoloured cats and salted lakes, of Crusaders' courts and Frankish forts, of Noah's ark and his vineyard, of black gardens and friendly mountains, and none more friendly than that distant neighbour there." He points to a silhouette with silver outline, discernible, but discernible only as to its distance.

"They too dreamt of fields of wheat, but beyond Ararat, to the west. They did dream of freedom, but not of people, of land. I tell you they are a stubborn people of Old Testament Prophets and Gospel writers, hearing only what they want to hear. When we spoke of jobs, they heard Job, and just as they dropped the 'S', so did they do of the 'X' that marked the spot of Marx, for instead, they heard only Mark, and closed their ears save only to hear the lions roar of the word, rather that, they bargained, and be the lone voice in the wilderness, than enjoy their godforsaken daily bread.

"What use for them the workers and words of the world united, when their world had already burnt to a cinder. Let the world burn and watch, these people will rise again, phoenix like. What need of the call of bread, peace, and land, in a land where the shadow of the call of the mute muezzin drowns out all other slogans. Bread, peace, land, they believe bred pieced land.

I saw the way the wind blew and quickly replaced Marx for Mark's gospel. How else do you save a people that would rather bare the neck than bend the knee?"

Ulyanov stands silently contemplative – no longer for him grandiose claims of paradise on earth, no more peddling dreams. He looks with childlike eyes on the brave new world, so alien to his vision.

"And what of you? Were you not a son of my cause? Did a blazing rain of bullets not blot out the sun of your commune on the Caspian's shores? Did you not die fighting in utopia's oil-drenched dawn? Is it so vice a name now the banner Bolshevik under which you too once upon a time marched? Was not the Bible beneath your pillow replaced with the same manifesto as mine? Did you not swear on your knees a new fealty to the masses and not The One?

"Comrade brother, I too dreamt your dreams, but look, I still am where once I was. The first to fall as martyr, this time I was the first to rise, saved. What use for utopian words such a people whose grandfathers turned swords into ploughshares, only then for grandsons to realise their ancestors were too hasty in seeing peace, and in such realisation, returned those same ploughshares into swords once again? When we gave them 'bread', they responded, 'give us freedom'; when we offered them 'peace', they demanded 'justice'; and when we offered them 'land', they cried in one voice, 'Karabagh!'

"Look not on me now, my once-upon-a-time brother, with socialist eyes, for long ago the raiment of communism did I discard. I stand instead before you dressed in folk garb: an Armenian born, an Armenian I remained. An Armenian from my mother's womb drawn, to being Armenian I returned, I was Armenian reclaimed!

"All these people ever heard of me was my martyrdom, and I, a martyr in my last, was forever doomed to so be an Armenian. This cursed, this damned, stubborn, blood-drenched race has a great affection for gallows, matched only by their love of martyrs. Deserts and mountains, wastelands, they call these places home. Exile for them is a fertile soil in which to grow like wheat, to in turn therein be cut down by an alien scythe. 'Better hell…' they cry single-mindedly, '…and hellfire scorch the bread they could be,' they say, then the wheat that is this people be ground, be kneaded, be baked, and rise. No, not for them a feast to prepare for, but instead their fate is for others to feast upon.

"You forget, Comrade Ulyanov, that this land was once Eden, that it was herein that once occurred The Fall. It is a fact that these stubborn Armenians have never forgotten, and having known paradise once already, had no further call for it in their land. Better to pluck the forbidden fruit of freedom, their logic ran, lest it wither on the branch and die.

"We had no chance of ever growing in their garden. Let it be black and bloody by our choice, was their sole want, 'our blood be upon us and our children!' was their response to our every counsel. With that they watched gleefully as we washed our hands and took our leave.

"They took the hammer of our banner and beat the sickle into a sabre and thus armed, marched to war, of our common flag they kept only the blood-like red.

"Now listen well, Brother Ulyanov, to their own folklore wisdom: a shepherd thought to tame the wolf by teaching him the alphabet, and begun thusly:

'A,' said the shepherd.

'Ass,' said the wolf.

'B,' said the shepherd.

'Buffalo,' said the wolf.

'C,' said the shepherd.

'Cow,' said the wolf.

"Understand well, they learn our language, but speak their own tongue.

"The great Shahenshahe Cyrus came to them and said: 'Come, fall into line, Persians become! Do so and you will be lords of all you survey!' They shook their heads, and said, 'We would rather die in droves.' "'Come be Greeks!' said Lord Alexander, and 'No!' they said in unison. 'We would rather our tortured script to your known curves.'

"Emperors came and promised to make them countrymen, friends even, if they would only lend them their ears and listen, but they suddenly all became deaf. Empires of Arabs, Turks, Iranians, and Russians, all pilgrims in this land, begged of them by swords-edge threat: turn away from whatever path you are hell bent on taking, and instead they bared their necks yet again.

"The rivers ran red with blood, and they poured forth ink.

"The very ground beneath them shook, and they stood rooted to the spot.

"Even the heavens, filled with every pantheon they ever worshipped, closed their doors with clouds to these people and they still knelt and prayed, burning their insufferable incense.

"For look at this land of theirs - what lessons can you learn other than to be forever, to be resolved and stand defiant. Now look at the greatest of these volcanic lumps..." and the Prophet Zartosht points to Ararat in the distance.

"This to them is as sacred as any word in any book. It is the navel to which every cord of everyone of them is tied. It is as tough as steel, which no scimitar or bayonet could ever hope cut. And what lies atop its peak, why the ark, a redoubt in which to hide away and outwit any deluge. Therein to await a new dawn, a new day, a new start which this valley forever promises to give forth.

"That is what we made for these people, Brother Ulyanov, not a utopia, no, no, that they already knew, but a new ark! We made true for them what was their greatest legend. We bolshie wickeds were just another Noah, and inside an ark we took in all they knew to be creation, and therein they waited for floodwaters to abate.

"See how they obeyed? See how they spread once more across the world? See how they planted even the vine once more, where once we said, 'Here, build factories', they said, 'No.' Not for them machinery - the grape they wanted, and on the vine to grow life and be drunk in between those times that their God called on them to make new sacrifices of flesh only that the aroma He find pleasing enough to pause the ever constant tragedy that is the tread of their theatre; injuncting them in such intermissions: 'be fruitful and multiply'.

"I have learnt anew the tales of old, rather than your tall tales told! I was but adrift across the endless ocean of ideas that covered this world, but when I sought dove-borne peace, it was atop this mountainside of my native land, I returned. For Armenian from my mother's womb I came, to Armenia, naked of my trappings I remained." The Prophet's sermon ends.

Ulyanov dumbfounded tries to speak but finds his stone tongue crumbling into gravel within the vacuous cave of his mouth. He tries to speak but the words falter, and he can only mumble the sound of rocks falling off a lonely hillside, a mumble to the audience of one, where once he roared in the direction of each compass point.

"Brother Shahumian, you sound like their damned priests!" Ulyanov manages to utter to the Prophet Zartosht, who responds:

"Verily I say that I am cut of that self-same cloth. No more the light bulb and books, no, manuscripts by candlelight for me instead. For try as I might to bury myself in causes greater, wander as I might in Moscow or Paris, or along Caspian shore, or beyond, I tell you, Armenia forever called me home, and I would rather here stand on sunlit plinth and be marvelled at than suffer your fate – a forgotten foolish one for only the feral creatures to piss on.

The Opium of the Masses

"I am martyr, and happy with that mantle. I am Jesus, betrayed by your kiss. I am Noah captaining the ark. I am now Saint Michael with flaming sword at the gates of this paradise casting you out - be gone, Ulyanov, oh foul cretin, be gone, and back to the backstreets, you peddler of wares, there return, fall from grace and in the index of bigger books and histories remain. Let your books be unread, your name in people's mouths a cursed refrain."

And with that, as Brother Ulyanov begins crumbling into a weathered mound of rubble resembling a ruin, the Prophet Zartosht turns his back on Ulyanov, who now, a quietened mound of chipped stone, is carved anew into nothing, by the biting words of scorn.

And as a midnight breeze blows through the quiet valley, the chanted liturgy can be heard wafting from the silent churches, whispering scripture lifted from vellum: *for false Christs, and false prophets shall rise, and shall shew signs and wonders to seduce…* and in this time, within the Godless Hour, there is no need for Ajami's presence, other devils are due their tithe of time.

VI.

The Parents

"'You have made your habitation in the icy cold; now warm and melt the freezing cold of your haughty conduct, submit to me and live in tranquillity in my empire wherever you please.' But Hayk responded to Bel's envoys with a firm no."

– Movses Khorenatsi

The Godless Hour draws on, creeping second by second, to its penumbra close. A caravan of stars is beginning to emerge in the heavens as this false night's dawn becomes nascent; a fake dawn, heralding only the promised approach of a true night to break the back of what time has hitherto stopped.

The Rose City will yet remain asleep, and with it, all therein still slumbering will yet be awake.

Knowing the hour of his play will soon be up, and lest he invoke the ire of the Almighty Father, Ajami fitfully begins returning the stones back to sleep atop their plinths, stirring his incantations in reverse, but all this is yet to be fully done, and not before allowing the final act of this tragic comedy to play out.

Ahead of the curtain fall, ending this playtime night, Ajami awakens the High Father of All.

Mother and Father

The High Father has arms of stony muscle and they hold taut a stringless bow, but as he awakens, he lets loose an arrow of imagination, the flight of which arcs over the Rose City to land at the foot of the High Mother of All. Replacing his bow to cross his chest, the High Father releases his feet from the rocky pillars into which they are embedded and sets out on a night-time walk to retrieve the arrow he half-awkwardly let go, muttering to himself through half-pursed stony lips: "It flew too far!"

The High Father walks through the city centre, pass the parched fountains, and then onwards, through the silent streets, silently treading in steady footsteps under still-leaved trees, oblivious to all and everything, just walking, to the onlooker appearing purposeless in so walking.

Walking until he sees the Stone Monk's lesson to the Titan, and caring not to learn, he carries on walking.

Walking beyond the conference of the Architect, the Maestro, and the Artist, still debating, he cares not to adjudicate amongst these sons, and walks on.

Walking past the battling bards and their entourage of squabbling poets, their cacophony interests him not, he keeps walking on.

Walking by, he pays no heed to the ceaseless gallop of the horserace, the clamber of hooves turns not his head, and so he walks on.

Walking with a deaf ear he passes by two communists, uttering nonsense, a nuisance, he walks past them on and up the deep steps of the Cascade Monument until his stone legs' muscles weaken and he comes to rest atop Yerevan's peak beside the waiting presence of the High Mother, his partner in otherwise lonely vigil. There, the two parents assemble, taking their place side-by-side to greet the false dawn of true night and with wakened eyes to see out the Godless Hour in survey of their children, the last remnant of which slumber still in this valley.

"Greetings, Mother of mine," says the High Father of All.

"Greetings, Father of All," replies the High Mother of All.

And they stare in silence at the pandemonium of the Rose City. After a patient pause, the Father turns to the Mother, and almost sighs his thoughts out loud:

"What hopes I had for my children. Such dreams, such, such dreams..." and the High Father shakes his head.

"As any parent would of any child born: high hopes and great expectations," says the High Mother.

"But all for nought," says the dejected High Father. "Look now how they squabble over the shape of words, the use of words, whether to sing songs or compose poems; see how they father and argue, the eternity of music, colour, and stone. And look here how they debate - isms and -ologies, whilst around them the enemy gathers forth for their slaughter.

"Their wise men talk with no action, their warriors charge the ranks only ever in a futile final sally, always courting dreams... and death... and damnation! And never content with the safety of just being, being far from the eyes of tyrants. Not enough, silence, no, not for them! Instead, they must chime their small voice to the chorus of nations, and therein be drowned out and silenced as nation follows nation to trample them." He shakes his head in bafflement and allows his face to carry the countenance of a broken soul, the look of someone inconsolable.

The All Mother turns to the All Father and with a caring hand strokes the nape of his neck reassuringly, but stone on stone grates, and sparks instead fly. "Speak of your bachelor days and faded glory, those better days will lift your spirits."

The High Father straightens his back and the mist of reminiscence glaze his eyes over. "I was a young man once. A young man in the plains of Akkad when mankind was itself young. Great were our numbers then, we sons of that plain that stretched before Babylon. We were giants too, heroes all, speaking the same tongue, and single-minded in every endeavour. Great were those days of sunshined peace.

"Amongst our ranked number a great vision was born; to build a great tower to the heavens and call upon God our heavenly Father and in His company, with Him converse, and after much idle and pleasant chat, ask simply: 'Why?'

"To this task we set pain and plan, work and virtue, and all were happy in pursuit. Equal and united in performing that one single task: to return to our heavenly Father. When any son of our cause fell to his death we paused not, but carried on building the tower, better a soul perished in our heavenward endeavour than one moment in time, for that wasted hour, we reserved the loudest of laments.

"But what man proposes, God disposes, for what fools were we to ever think heaven was attainable. For in our task we succeeded only in invoking God's ire, and set amongst us a pestilence of tongues, so that where once we were of one voice and single-minded, now we were as sheep baahing at each other, a babel of languages broke us into fragments, a great conversation of tongues, unable to be understood, let alone make common cause. We were all voices crying in the wilderness.

"Seeing that both the cause and the land were lost I found there in the ruins of our endeavour kith and kin of one tongue and though we were too few to build the tower, we were happy to meet and understand.

"We were but a few score in number, and knowing that the great plain had become a ground for the nations to break against each other, I gathered to my side those who would heed my call and understand my pledge to lead them to a new home.

"I found them such a home, one in a shaded valley within the foothills of that mountain where our grandfather landed after the Great Flood. We were not so wicked as to stay among evildoers, and so we would escape wickedness in retreating to that same valley where those who escaped evil before found their respite. We did not flee, but had returned! Returned to live apart from those who would rather barter for empires, or seek better gods by their own endeavours, than accept what was their allotted portion, and know that there is only one above all. Not a promise for kingdoms or empires did I give, not one pledge that our loving land would surpass all others, no great gods did I invoke, nor did I set our broken backs to some vain vision of grandeur. My promise was but a simple pledge: that we would return and live alone in our valley, therein to live in the shade of mountains, retire from the world, and know only peace.

"There peace did reign for a time, until the hour was due when the tyrant Bel heard of us. His was a dream of uniting all men, not to the lofty task of tower raising, but to the sloth of empire.

"He martialled forth his followers, now an army, and marched forth from the plains of Akkad to the valleys of Ararat and there to demand my, his own kinsman's, submission.

"We would not bend the knee, nor bare the neck, but I, as their leader, led three hundred to meet the enemy. Our only oath this, and this alone, to defend our mountain home and not submit, not for glory, not for praise, or for fighting's sake fight. Not for us to roll up our sleeves on feast days and bare our arms to show scars and talk in throwaway words of battles old – no! We resolved only to die in freedom, or save that small valley that we knew to be our apportioned lot, that sweet land we christened: 'Enough'.

"By one swift arrow and much flurry of swords, Bel was dispatched, and to our homes in our valley we returned to sire sons and see grandsons, to be fruitful and multiply, and to my stewardship, they, my brethren gifted me this land, not a king mind, no, but a first among equals, and all to be brothers together; in arms, in feats, in endeavour, but brothers forever! And so the land Enough took my name: Hayastan!

"But history births legends, and legends must in turn nurse myths, and in so doing, meaning is lost: whether this happened, or not, becomes manna for scholars too drunk with books. Too much toing and froing with words sacrifices meaning to debate, whose due is that meaning, that most fragile thing, alas, lost, and with it, any example to follow.

"I led these people to a valley and said: 'Let here be home. Here be content', and offered them what is now beneath your feet. 'Dream not of anything beyond,' I said, but they did not listen.

"Look now, All Mother, look at your children, scattered and flung like chaff dreaming of lost lands, trying to build towers to God instead of being content with this valley, their due portion, from which they advanced, only to retreat in turn. They call me leader, but will not follow my lead – ask me now, how am I to be a proud parent?"

The All Mother holds the All Father's hands in her own gentle clasp and speaks reassuringly. "Not all dreams are destined to wake into reality. Not everything amounts to something. Look now with fresh eyes upon this valley, take a maternal gaze filled with maternal love in place of the expectant father's sight. True, by example you led, truer still you stand ready to defend, but think back to our nuptial night. Do you recall our wedding day? When on that night we took our vows?"

"Of course! A blessed night of holy covenant: what was united cannot be divided," he replies.

"Oh, but it was so much more! You were a young man then, of steel, not stone, and moustached, yet to be bearded. Do you remember?

"I remember the day you took leave of your pedestal atop this lofty peak and took off that great overcoat, so warm was that day...yes, I remember it now, you shaved the moustache of the kremlin highlander and were bare cheeked, stripped to the waist!

"Stone replacing steel, you took up a new position, right here." She gently stamps her foot before continuing, "Resolutely minded and with attending, watchful eyes, you drew back your bow string until taut stiff in place, arrow at the ready, ever ready to defend your progeny and shoot down any enemy that dared defy the borders of what remained of your children's homeland. You became a wandering father, half recalled home, and yet along the frontier forever roaming there, to keep watch for the return of Bel. Defender of the hearth you were, and as you roamed, you called out to me to leave the bridal chamber and take your place attending the fires of home.

"We agreed our children needed no more martial valour or manly virtue, but instead here in this valley redoubt, valuable, maternal embrace. We agreed that the family we reared together would know peace. No longer for them, a bow hastily drawn, nor eagle eyes to scan the horizon for would-be nemesis, no, instead the maternal gaze to look upon and have looked down upon them. To know a mother's love and tenderness, and thereunder bask, knowing the fierce mother with sword drawn stands ready to defend, whilst the father hither roams, but not too far from home, that was all our children ever needed, all they ever wanted: parents to charge away bears and wolves, tsars and shahs.

"Were we bad parents? Did I all too late come here and stand with sword drawn ready to defend after too much bloody playtime? I console myself that it was under my sight that came artists and poets, musicians and architects, that here on this night, my brood argues, bickers, and tittle-tattles.

"They all were weaned by my breast, and in my bosomed embrace, raised; our small people, our children, once again knowing peace at the feet of their too absent mother. And in this fortress, I made home, they flowered and grew. As I stood, beneath the fabled mountain wondering, I saw you as Noah, offering sacrifices, drinking of wild vines, in shamed revelry given, and I, Naamah, the hearth tending, slowly the home did mend, both of us waiting on the other side of the mountain for the return when the floodwaters of history had abated; all the while, this last, most loyal valley, swelled pregnant with expectant birth.

"I gave truth through my actions to that biblical injunction: 'be fruitful and multiply', and so they did, their numbers grew, and fathers knew grandparents and grandchildren in turn, generations grew and lived safely and knew each other too, till friends mourned at gravesides, rather than be buried beside them in unripe years and too great numbers.

"But you lived babbling on, trying to gather your sons scattered abroad, those ingrate waywards, placed all upon, about, and across the face of the earth, so that the limit of one's exile bordered the beginning of the other's. Those orphans that would not come home were lost sheep, I told you so, and yet you insisted on being their shepherd, though a flock from their number you could not create. For lost souls cannot be gathered lest they cease to be lost, and some do not wish to be found, regardless of how hard you look."

"But what a little brood," says the All Father "Where I led tribes and clans, here is at most a litter."

"A fragment from a fragment remains - be grateful! Think back on the tale of the lioness and the fox.

"It is said the fox remarked it unremarkable that the lioness birthed a single cub, given that the vixen herself brings forth cubs with each litter, but said the lioness, 'Mine is a lion cub, whereas you bring forth a brood of foxes.'"

"Better they amounted to nothing, than disappoint so," says the All Father.

"Nothing comes from nothing!" replies the All Mother.

"Better that then!" retorts the All Father.

"Hush now your melancholy. Pack it away. Let it be done. Let it be gone. This land needs no more patriarchs to peddle dreams, and certainly no more talk of times past, or even futures forward, none of this does it want for. It needs only the loving maternal embrace, the womb's warmth to return to, and perhaps be reborn again.

"Go now with your bow and feats of arms, back to the border and roam with foot and eye. Keep there your watch for the enemy, should he ever come, if he does, then let loose a volley of arrows in defence of this valley, sound the bell, and to arms once more call your sons. For if Bel is what you hope to see, then it is Bel which you will find. But remember this, these children of ours need no more enemies, of them, they have had their fill, and if no enemies, then so too need they no heroes.

"Let no more statues be called from stone, nor cast forth from iron forge.

"Let no more men of stature come, and finally say end to dreams of loss and legends, I will not even tell them these when bedtime comes.

"Let them all look inward to the peak upon which I stand, and let this summit in place of any other suffice.

"Let every son be as though my bridegroom, and every daughter, my handmaiden come. Let the hem of my skirt be as a great tent under which all our children gather.

"Let them say God has abandoned them, but here we have a goddess, who never averted her gaze.

"Let every poet sing my praises and writers of my non-acts write dumb.

"Let I be as leviathan, a giant over all the tyrants who have so tormented this blighted valley, a force not so easily overcome.

"Let those that will return follow you to this land, but here find rest and a mother's embrace and a father's steady hand.

"Let the weary come home knowing that their mother awaits with opened arms ready to greet the weary in need of rest, for in me there be a mother, a love unquestioning, unquenching, merely calling out: 'Come home!'

"But let those who ever roam and see not here a home to return and settle, then let those sons and daughters be as though forever lost, forever looking over their shoulder for Bel to embrace them in his Babel, or dedicate themselves to towers to heaven, or some other such stupid fable.

"For whoever fears tyrants, tyrants they will find, and no more does this land need of such a kind.

"Now go hither and leave us this pregnant pause, return not, for look, the dawn casts its shadow on the dusk we have known. Let us leave in silence, you to be watchful, forever calling that they return, those doomed to be unknown, and leave me to be caring, matriarchal, for all who remain, ingathered, in peace, at home. Together we shall be as two parents forever apart, calling our children to home depart, and from same home, never again part.

"Let the rest that might be said remain unspoken, for the hour draws nigh and the love we share is not ours to keep between us, but as failing and faltering as the night, so it is, and for our children's sake given. Think not of rights and wrongs, of what could have been; instead rest now here once again and be grateful for the nightmares not seen.

"Let us agree that when next time heaven decrees, we again awaken and you come hither, you do so to come and rest atop my bosom, and we will then together look with pride on the children of this valley and sing praises in place of lament. Go now lover mine with love's blessing upon your lips, sleep in peace, dream not of past glories, but new things that might come to be. Your dreams send to my womb to be known and see what child might be born, or else, defy, and let your empty head be this country's gravestone."

The Great Father takes his leave of the Great Mother and with reluctant tread comes down from the mountain, atop which the Great Mother returns to her pose of defensive posture. Past the Architect returning to his plans with out-splayed hands, and the Ebony Maestro atop his plinth, the Alabaster One striking once more a painter's pose. The Bard falls sighingly silent before his three muses. The Moustache stands once more wistfully distilling the night, and the poets and the Oaken Priest return too to their corners. The Stone Monk packs away his lessons and returns to that repository of books, whilst the Titan mournfully walks past what remains of his empire, back to the pedestal tomb of his kingdom. The pantheon of the Rose City all return to their places in the firmament to sleep the eternal sleep of stone, just as the All Father takes his final step back into his hewn known repose.

Atop his perch on the ledge of the Opera House, Ajami laughs and cackles at his night's play.

Dawn breaks to chase away the Godless Hour, and in its entourage bears the promise of daybreak's dew, whilst sunlight choruses with birdsong to make morning, everything is as though new.

His nightly play to an end comes just as Ajami calls an end to his revelry.

He takes his leave of the Rose City and the valley in which it is nestled. New playgrounds await him and his nightly game, for other cities too are too burdened by

The Progress of Peace

history cast in the permanence of works of stone, and they too await his theatre. Ajami laughs one final cackle - it sounds as though a rook greets daybreak. The Godless Hour comes to a stop and the Rose City is reclaimed by its denizens who fill it with a new panoply of muses, and where in new tragedy and new gossip drown out the secrecy of yesterday's night, and those even further before.

In the central square, a single dove begins its descent, and sweeping low comes to land upon the central pedestal where once a statue stood by way of perch, but finding nought the little bird takes to flight again. Not for it this parched land with no statues on which to stand, just sleeping giants with heads of stone that beat against each other and in unison chime a good morning to the dawn of the Godless Hour's end.

Dramatis Personae

Titan - Tigran the Great
Stone Monk - Mesrop Mashtots
Moustachioed Man - William Saroyan
Diminutive Bard / Bard / Chanson - Charles Aznavour
Alabaster One - Martiros Saryan
Architect - Hovhannes Tumanyan
Colossus / Ebony Maestro - Aram Khachaturian
Gnarled Old Man - Karabala
Goatlike One - Avetik Isahakyan
The Nose / Torso-less Nose - Yegishe Charents
Bard of Three Muses - Sayat Nova
Oaken Priest - Komitas
Daredevil of Sassun / The Myth - Sasuntsi Davit
The Legend - Vartan Mamikonean
Fedayi / Zoravor - Antranik
Marshall of Karabagh - Marshall Bagramyan
Prophet Zartosht - Stepan Shahumian
Ulyanov - Vladimir Lenin
The High Father - Haik Nahapet
The High Mother - Mayr Hayastan

Acknowledgements

This book was written in several locations, but mostly in a little corner of II Floor, a cafe in downtown Yerevan where without the staff's music choices and readiness to give me yet another pot of tea, this book would not have come about - thank you all! Thank you too to Araz ("Araxi") who made me take breaks for knefeh. Also, to all those who provided helpful feedback, edits and mined my references. To Ara Sarafian for his patience in getting this all to fruition. Most of all thank you to Melanie whose encouragement and support led to this idea ever seeing light outside of my notebooks, and whose presence and company, this book, and I, both owe a great debt.

www.ingramcontent.com/pod-product-compliance
Lightning Source LLC
LaVergne TN
LVHW091008080826
845145LV00003B/1176

* 9 7 8 1 9 0 9 3 8 2 6 8 8 *